SO-AVL-359

WITHDRAWN
Damaged, Obsolete, or Surplus
Jackson County Library Services

DATE DUE   OCT 0 6

SEP 0 3 2013		
SEP 1 0 2013		
GAYLORD		PRINTED IN U.S.A.

In
State
of
Becoming

In
State
of
Becoming

SIMON VAN DER HEYM

Ivy
House
Publishing Group

www.ivyhousebooks.com

JACKSON COUNTY LIBRARY SERVICES
MEDFORD OREGON 97501

PUBLISHED BY IVY HOUSE PUBLISHING GROUP
5122 Bur Oak Circle, Raleigh, NC 27612
United States of America
919-782-0281
www.ivyhousebooks.com

ISBN: 1-57197-443-1
Library of Congress Control Number: 2004117851

© 2006 Simon van der Heym

All rights reserved, which includes the right to reproduce
this book or portions thereof in any form whatsoever
except as provided by the U.S. Copyright Law.

*This is a work of fiction. Names, characters, places, and incidents
are either a product of the author's imagination or are used
fictitiously. Any resemblance to actual events or persons, living
or dead, is entirely coincidental.*

Printed in the United States of America

To the God within all of us.

FOREWORD

Stillness is the experience of many sounds.

After silence, that which comes closest to the inexpressible is the silent sound of lingering musical notes.

After the silent sound of lingering music notes, that which comes closest to the inexpressible is the silent sound of the midnight wind on a summer's eve.

After the silent sound of the midnight wind on a summer's eve, that which comes closest to the inexpressible is the silent touching of two souls in divine love.

After the silent touching of two souls in divine love, that which comes closest to the inexpressible is the silent sound of the dead on a distant battlefield.

After the silence of the dead on a distant battlefield, that which comes closest to the inexpressible is the silence of Universal Love.

After the silence of Universal Love, that which comes closest to the sound of the inexpressible is the silence of Divine Peace.

— Simon van der Heym
May 28, 2003

PROLOGUE

Why did I entitle this book *In State of Becoming*?

When an artist lovingly mixes two or more paint colors on his pallet to create a different shade or hue, he experiments, to get just the right tinge that only he can envision in his mind's eye. When, after a long harsh winter, we sense that nature is in a state of becoming, we know that spring is not far off and that everything is in transition. Soon, all will be new and lush and fresh again.

The love story you are about to read, in a sense is like that.

Although I have had no medical training, I do believe that our bodies produce chemicals that activate and stimulate our brain in order to create thoughts, either positive, neutral or negative, which in turn significantly affects our moods and people who suffer from a Bi-Polar condition experience considerable mood swings due to a chemical imbalance. But, do we need to label this condition an illness? Their state of becoming may be a constant struggle to grow and is an expression of their own uniqueness.

Some days, our own thoughts illuminate our minds like beacons, shining lights in places we've never visited before. Sometimes rational and lucid, sometimes contrarily. Some are filled with inspiration or emotions, some are sweet like the tender kisses from those we love. Which is dream and which is reality?

We form beliefs—alliances, political or otherwise—because we are social creatures. Which perceptions do we honor, as we walk along our personal paths of evolution, immersing ourselves in this ocean of life, choosing how wet we let ourselves get—or, staying safe and dry, away from the tidal wave of options, not yet able or willing to commit as we play our eternal "what if head games," since these are less painful than the realities of life.

What if there are other alternatives to avoiding the threat of insurgents or terrorists? What if we could stamp out world poverty and in so doing, give credence to our collective universal needs. *In State of Becoming* is about all of us who are in this process of transition—this evolutionary process.

* * *

After the silent touching of two souls in divine love, that which comes closest to the inexpressible is the silence of the dead in a distant city or country.

After the silence of the dead, that which comes closest to the inexpressible is the silence of universal love for each other.

After the silence of universal love, that which comes closest to the inexpressible is the silence of divine peace.

* * *

We are all connected—one people, one universe, one God—and what we do to others, we also do to ourselves. Is it time to begin shifting our collective consciousness?

Chapter
ONE

It was snowing. Not a heavy snow mind you, it wasn't quite cold enough for that. It was only early in November but the weather had turned colder almost overnight from the warm and balmy late summer temperatures they had been enjoying.

Eric was standing in front of the big kitchen windows which overlooked the sprawling gardens of the house in King City where he had found temporary sanctuary.

The snow was of the wet variety but it had covered the grass and the trees with a white powdery blanket. He looked at the falling snow and sighed deeply. He couldn't quite decide what this sigh was all about or where it came from. Was it one of relief, with perhaps a bit of melancholy thrown in for good measure? Was he expressing sadness on this early Sunday morning? The sadness which he felt in his heart and his soul about the love of a women he no longer could love? Or was it relief because his six months old marriage to Michelle had finally come to an end?

Oddly enough, the white snow made him feel like he, as well as nature, were beginning anew: fresh and clean and white.

A clean sweep from the horrendous error he had made only six short months ago. They had all warned him not to get married but he hadn't wanted to listen.

He had told himself that his brother Joseph was incapable of understanding. Joseph's enormous ego would not allow him to think about anything beyond his own basic need to always be right.

His younger brother Jonathan had just suffered a stroke and wasn't quite himself yet. He hadn't gotten back to the point where he was capable of reasoning things out and so he took the line of least resistance by agreeing with whatever Joseph had said.

Eric remembered vividly the discussions he had with Sybille, his sister and her husband. They had always been his favorite family members and he had been very surprised, that they too had voiced a very strong opposition and had many negative opinions about his decision to marry Michelle.

Yet, they had offered him the sanctuary of their home, now that he had become temporary homeless.

"All I have ever wanted," he had explained to them, "is to enjoy the balance of my years in happiness and peace. To take pleasure in a little traveling with Michelle, while I am still healthy enough to enjoy it." His health had continued to improve steadily.

"Why get married?" they all had said. "Haven't you learned enough from your previous mistakes?" They all knew of course that every time he became divorced, it had cost him plenty.

Eric had done well enough in the business world, but when it came to finding a life's partner, he had failed miserably.

When he had turned sixty-five, he had retired and moved with his family to Florida, mainly to escape from the harsh Canadian winter weather, like so many other Canadian snowbirds.

They however could never become snowbirds because of Jamie, their daughter.

Jamie had just turned six when Eric had retired. She had been his whole life, apart from his successful corporation, which, over the many years, he had built from the ground up.

When Eric and Jane had discussed his retirement, they both had wanted Jamie to attend and remain in one school permanently, and so traveling back and forth from Toronto to Florida for the winter months was out of the question.

He had felt so bone tired then, he remembered. Even the year before his retirement, he had not been feeling well.

Still, he was surprised, when a short time after his retirement, during a routine physical examination, he was told that he had cancer. It had gone too far, they had said. Surgery was now out of the question.

He had spent eight agonizing months going from medical guru to guru trying to discover what his options were and after he had exhausted every possibility, he finally decided to follow his oncologist's advise.

They administered hormone injections to shrink the tumor down, then, a lengthy radiation process and finally, radioactive pellet implants. For some reason he hadn't wanted to question, they had called it "The Sandwich Method."

He had felt a great deal more ill after his treatments because of the damage to his insides which inevitably occurred, but they had succeeded in arresting the cancer.

Eric had never been quite sure of this. Had it been the treatments or was it because he personally had changed a great deal? At any rate, he had been given a second chance and he had started to take better care of himself. He had changed his diet and his eating habits and he had started looking at the meaning of life in quite a different way.

Before all of this had happened, Eric had never been a religious person. He knew about God of course, but he, like so many of his peers, had believed that God was some sort of a supernatural overseer of life.

He'd been born a Jew, but now, after his ordeal, he had started to think differently about God. His philosophies began to shift and he began to think of God, not as some deity up somewhere in the heavens, sitting there and over-looking everything, but he gradually began to see God as the God-self in him and in all the other creatures that inhabited his universe.

A year after his implants, Jane decided she did not like being retired after all, and they began to grow apart.

Eric was never able to determine if she had difficulties in adapting to his new and changed philosophical outlook of life or, was it because she was so much younger than him, that the retirement issue had become the reason for their separation and the inevitable divorce which followed.

Philosophical concepts, he decided, had never been one of his wife's stronger suits.

But selfishly, Eric had never bothered to ask. His pride or his ego would not allow this. He could not or would not turn back the clock. He just couldn't see himself making his transition in reverse.

She had said that she missed her work and her career as a fabric designer and she eventually asked him for a divorce.

At the time, when he had agreed to the divorce, Eric did not realize what she apparently had wanted all along. Later, he discovered that she had planned to return to Toronto, to go back to work for Eric's former company which had been sold to his employee group. A truth she had failed to share with him when she had asked him for the divorce.

The new president, who Eric had trained personally, made her a partner, when Jane decided to buy back into the company, using part of the lump sum of the very generous settlement Eric had paid her. He hadn't minded this, after all, his Jamie would have everything she ever needed.

Jane had also requested custody of Jamie when she filed for the divorce and Eric had not opposed her on this. He had of course not expected then that Jane would move back to Toronto, taking Jamie along with her and out of his life.

For a long time after their departure, he had been devastated and he would frequently travel back to Toronto to spend time with his daughter.

Their bonding, which was so evident before Jamie had moved back with her mother, seemed to be getting lost between them and the rebuilding of his relationship with his daughter did not seem to go at all well.

With Jane working full time now at the plant, Eric decided that he should seriously consider moving back to Toronto in order for him to contribute to and to play a more meaningful role in his daughter's upbringing. After all, there was nothing of great importance to keep him in Florida now.

It was during these sometimes agonizing deliberations, when he met and fell in love with Michelle. At least he thought he had, or was he just too vulnerable and lonely?

Chapter
TWO

They met at a seminar. It had been organized by the Religious Science Center. Ever since Jane and Jamie had left, Eric had been going to the Center almost every Sunday morning. It wasn't really a church, actually Eric had little use for organized religions. The Center was more like a community of people who shared the same kind of philosophies that he had adopted.

From the very first moment that he had entered their humble and simple worship space and when he observed how people interacted with each other in warm and loving ways, he had felt a strong bonding, which for him had been lacking with other religious convictions.

These people seemed to live and act out that the God of their understanding was within each one of them. There was a special connectedness which seemed to say, "Whatever I do for you, I do for me as well, for when I embrace you, I also embrace myself." As a result, whenever he visited the Center, he received his share of hugs and perhaps for the first time in his life, he felt truly loved, liked he really belonged.

He had gotten to know the minister quite well. Eric had guessed that Nora was a woman in her mid fifties, who dressed well, but quite simply and who didn't need a lot of make-up to look attractive.

He liked the way she talked with him. Very natural and personable and she was one of those highly intelligent women who didn't need to put on any airs about how smart they really were.

Eric had met many very nice, warm and loving people at the Center and he had joined their men's group. They would usually get together once every two weeks and would discuss various worthwhile charitable programs that they might be interested in pursuing.

During one of the Center's Saturday seminars, which had been organized by one of the members Eric had made friends with, and which was planned to teach people to better deal with their grieving and sadness, he was introduced to a woman he had not previously seen there at the Center.

Michelle was a very attractive woman, he guessed in her early fifties, but she cried almost consistently, which made her mascara run and left ugly streaks on her otherwise beautiful face.

He felt sorry for her at first and he couldn't imagine what had made her so very unhappy. Later he discovered that she had been in a seven year long relationship that had ended rather badly without any chance for a reconciliation.

During the lunch break, he and several of his friends went out to lunch and Eric hadn't realized that many of those who attended the seminar had brought their own lunch.

The restaurant had been quite crowded and they had to wait a long time before their orders were served. While they waited, they started to discuss some of the topics they had covered that morning. They got into it a little more deeply than they intended and as a result had lost track of time.

When they returned, the others had been waiting for them for a while and some of their stares had been a little less than loving or cordial.

Of course, he had apologized for their tardy return and for keeping the group waiting. He explained, "Some of us were unaware that we should have brought our own lunch. Perhaps it might have been a good idea to indicate this on the brochure."

Michelle responded immediately on behalf of the group. "Perhaps you should have looked a little closer. It was definitely indicated on the brochure," she said.

Eric was a little embarrassed by her attitude and her somewhat rude mannerisms, but he good-naturedly explained that he had only seen the announcement of the seminar on the bulletin board and therefore had missed this information which had in all likelihood been noted on the reverse side.

He was however a little surprised that her tears and that terrible sadness he had seen earlier, had been so quickly replaced with this somewhat more aggressive behavior. He had also noticed that she had re-done her make-up and when he looked at her more closely, he realized, that she was quite a stunning looking woman.

Later that afternoon she again burst into tears and he, for the second time that day, began to feel a little sorry for her. What was it, he wondered, that could make a person feel so very sad?

They met again quite by accident the following Sunday at the Center, after the service. Nora's homily had been particularly moving that morning and as had become his custom, Eric gave her a big hug and complemented her for the beauty and eloquence by which she had delivered her message.

Usually, the members of the congregation met for coffee and cake in an area specially designated for that purpose—a place where people could talk and enjoy each other's company.

That is where he ran into her again, and once again the tears were flowing so tragically, that Eric felled compelled to give her a hug and he said, "Things can't possibly be as bad as all that."

She looked at him. Her eyes were beautiful, he realized, but terribly sad. And again, the tears had started flowing from her almost dry, but still glisteningly moist eyes.

She didn't respond, but her eyes told him, "How could you possibly know anything about that?"

One of Eric's friends joined them. Ruth had attended the same seminar and apparently, she and Michelle seemed to know each other.

They talked for a while and then Eric asked both of them to lunch. He was however aware of the facts that it might look very strange for him to go to a restaurant with two ladies in tow, with one of them bawling her eyes out. So rather than going to a restaurant he suggested that they come to his house and he promised to make them one of his gourmet salads.

Eric's house was a small but nicely appointed two story, with a beautiful view overlooking his pool and the sizable lake beyond. A pleasant place, conducive to good conversation where one can kick back and feel very much at peace with the world outside.

Both women felt immediately comfortable. Michelle had stopped crying and she seemed much more at ease. She gradually began to take part in a lively debate, which was going on between him and Ruth.

Several hours later, Ruth announced that she had to

leave but Michelle did not seem to be in any great hurry to go. They talked until late that afternoon and Eric, who had planned to make one of his favorite salmon dishes, asked her to stay for dinner.

She accepted and they cooked and talked until about nine that evening. They exchanged phone numbers and then Michelle excused herself to drive back to her own house in Clearwater.

During their conversations, she had explained to Eric that she wanted to put her place up for sale. "But the house is in such a mess," she explained, "I would need to do some painting first, before I can put it on the market.

"I have not worked for some time," she said, "so this will have to wait until I can get some part-time work. Then I can afford to buy the paint I need and get the place more presentable. I really don't like living in Florida. I can't stand the summers here, the air is so still that I often feel like I am suffocating from the heat."

Eric secretly promised himself that he would speak to his men's group to see if they thought that this would be a worthwhile work project for them to undertake.

He walked her to her car and gave her directions for a shortcut to get out of the gated community. They hugged and he promised to phone soon.

She opened the windows of her car to let out the hot and humid air and Eric bent down and said through the window, "I have a sailboat, at a marina near the beach, perhaps you would like to go sailing sometime."

"I think I would like that very much," she said as she drove off in the direction of the gates.

Chapter
THREE

He had decided to wait a few weeks before calling her. He did not want to seem overly anxious. The days dragged on and he finally gave up after the fifth day. He called and had to leave a message. This annoyed him and he didn't know why it should. For some reason he could not understand, he had been sure that she would be home when he called.

He did not hear from her for several days. Then, she finally returned his call on Saturday, when he had been out. He had been working on his boat that entire day. When he returned home, he listened to her message and he immediately phoned her back.

"Hello Michelle," he said. "Sorry to phone you back so late, but I only minutes ago returned from working on my boat. How are you doing?"

She said she felt better. "I haven't cried for the whole week. I am sorry you had to see me that way, Eric, but I have been very depressed lately. It must be a hormone imbalance or something."

Eric muttered something dumb, like that he did not know much about stuff like that. He asked her if she was going to the Center tomorrow.

"Yes," she responded. "Why are you asking?"

"I was hoping that perhaps you might like to go for a walk on the beach tomorrow after services. It is going to be a beautiful day, but it will be much too windy to go sailing."

"I would like that very much, Eric" she said. "Should I bring us something for lunch?"

"No thanks" he answered. "Let's grab a bite out before we go. It will be much too windy to eat on the beach. Unless of course you happen to love sandy sandwiches. I would far prefer to stop at Applebee's before we head out."

"Sounds like a plan to me," she said. "So I will see you tomorrow at church, ok?" Then they hung up. She, probably because she couldn't think of anything further to say, and he because he did not want to give her a chance to change her mind.

Eric did not sleep well that night. He kept waking to see what time it was. Finally, at four in the morning he decided to get out of bed. As he looked outside, through his bedroom window, he saw that the moon had created a lovely silvery bright pattern on his pool and on the lake beyond.

The golf course was just a few steps away from his front door and Eric felt the need to go for a good hard jog on the golf-cart path that was adjacent to the fairways. He usually jogged there early most every morning, well before the golfers got there. He had always loved to see the world wake up and it often seemed to him that somewhere up in the east, someone was slowly raising a torch to light up the sky, like foreplay, somewhat ahead of when the sun finally and in its full glory became once again fully visible.

Every time he saw this spectacle played out, he became aware of a special feeling within him, and he would once again become aware of the very connection between him and nature, between him and his universe.

Sometimes he would spot a few deer, playing in the dewed grass in the early morning sun. Then, he would realize that these lovely and graceful creatures too would feel that same special kind of connectedness.

He was almost convinced that on this early morning, with a full moon bathing the fairways in a cool iridescent light, he would surely meet up with some of them.

When he began his jog, he realized how fortunate he was to be awake. At this early morning hour, with this very special illumination, everything looked quite different. At first, it was difficult for him to find expression for what he saw. Then, he realized it. Without sunlight, all colors seemed much less intense, less brilliant, with a cool, almost aloof beauty that he had never been aware of before.

He rested for a moment at a particularly lovely spot. There, in the thick forest, which in many areas bordered the fairways, the moonlight seemed to have illuminated, what could only be described as an almost invisible pathway. It was as though the viewer was beckoned to follow this path that seemed to lead deeper and deeper into an ever-darkening forest.

Then, out of nowhere they appeared. There were at least six of them. A buck, three or four fawns and a doe. They looked at him curiously, but without fear, he thought.

Eric tried to control his laboring breathing. He did not want to frighten them away. Finally, after what seemed like a long time, the buck and the fawns disappeared down the invisible pathway, but the doe remained. Her soft and moist large brown eyes looked into his for some considerable time and he, at that very moment was convinced that she was trying to communicate something to him. Something too valuable to miss.

Oh, how he wished then that he had the ability to hear what it was she tried to convey to him.

Finally, she too disappeared gracefully into the direction the others had gone.

He stood there, for a time transfixed, wondering what it was that the doe had wanted so desperately to impart to him. He was sure that he would find out in due course.

Then he shook his head, as one would do when a dream does not make a lot of sense and he continued his run, while the faintest of daylight just began to appear on the eastern horizon, announcing to the world that a new day was yet about to begin again.

Eric looked forward to this newness, which he knew would be the beginning of a wonderful and new life for him. Once again, a new beginning.

Chapter
FOUR

He spotted her at the Center during worship services, but he had been a few minutes late and she was already seated. There were no seat available next to her and Eric sat down quietly on one of the back rows. He tried to concentrate on Nora's sermon but unlike other times, his eyes kept wandering back to where Michelle was sitting.

He liked her hair, he decided, the way it was done. It was streaked and casually brushed back. It seemed to be naturally wavy. Since he sat behind her and well to her right, he was able to admire her profile. Her facial structure had softly sculpted lines and her thick black lashes were visible even from this distance. Again he was struck by her lovely features.

After service, he went over to where she was seated. He hugged her and wished her a happy Sunday. Together they went to the great room for coffee and to chat with some of their acquaintances.

One of her male friends approached them and introduced himself to Eric. With some excitement he told Michelle that he had just seen Charlie in the men's room.

Visible nervous now, Michelle explained to Eric, that she and Charlie had just broken off a seven year long relationship.

She added, "Eric, he is the reason why I have been so very depressed lately. I ran into him a few weeks ago at a meeting and that was the first time I had actually seen him cry. The last few years our relationship has been off and on and I do not think that he wants to continue to see me."

Eric thought to himself: Apparently, Michelle seems to think that it is important for a man to be able to express his feelings, such as crying, in public. She had made a special point of mentioning this, although he didn't know why, nor could he imagine why she felt that way. She didn't elaborate as to why he had shown so much emotion and he wondered if she thought it was because they had broken up, or had there been some other reason for his sadness.

While he pondered this, Charlie came over to where they were standing and Michelle introduced them. To Eric, it appeared that he seemed a little uneasy at seeing them together. They talked for while and Michelle said that Charlie was a computer technician at Honeywell. Eric commented that he had always been fascinated by people with such skills and said to Charley, "Maybe at some time in the future you might be able to give me some ideas on how to update my computer?" Charlie said he would be pleased to do so.

Eric, who by now, for reasons not altogether clear to him, was anxious to leave, said to Michelle, "We'd better be going to Applebee's or else the place will be packed with the usual after-church Sunday crowd."

He purposely did not want to include the others and he secretly hoped that they would not invite themselves along. He apologized for leaving so soon. As they left, they hurriedly said goodbye to Nora and to some of their other acquaintances.

As they exited the building, they were greeted by pleasantly warm sunshine, the clearest of blue skies imaginable and strong but balmy breezes.

Michelle drove a '97 Ford Escort and they decided to take Eric's new Volvo convertible and leave her car in the lot.

It was such a gorgeous afternoon for early October. The heavy humidity, normally still very prevalent during that time of the year, had all but disappeared and although the winds were quite gusty at times, the sun would often and playfully show herself from behind the occasional storm clouds. It was one of those ideal Florida days to drive a convertible and Eric was most anxious to make a good impression.

They were able to get a table at Applebee's without having to wait too terribly long and they talked about everything and nothing at all, the way people do when they have only met a short time ago, and want to just highlight, without getting too deeply involved in any subject. Eric was careful to avoid any reference to Michelle's past relationship with Charlie. Again, he didn't exactly know why. What was it that made him so concerned about her issues with Charlie?

After lunch, they drove across the Belle Air causeway to Gulf Boulevard and turned right to Sand Key Park. Eric loved Sand Key beach. He thought it was one of the most beautiful beaches he had ever been to.

His sailboat was docked at a marina just across the bridge from there and whenever he slept on board, he would often make the hike across the bridge and would take an early morning jog along the beach.

It was a windy and cool day, with one of the first cold fronts of the season passing through.

He liked her common-sense respect for the weather, the

way she had dressed for it. She wore overalls, a thick-yarned coarsely knitted pink sweater and a pair of beige Hush-Puppie ankle boots. "Fashionably casual" he had called it, when he complimented her on her outfit.

Eric had taken his new digital camera along and they both took turns in taking lots of interesting action shots of wind-blown faces and hair, eyes squinting against the wind and sand with the waves crashing on the sandy beach as a background. They walked hand in hand, talking mostly about nature and spirituality and smiled a lot at each other.

Michelle had the most radiant smile imaginable. When she did, which was often that day, her whole face would light up and her flashing white teeth would have made an outstanding commercial for any brand of toothpaste.

She is so different now, he thought, from the way she had been when he had first met her, when he had felt so very sorry for her.

She talked about her house and said that she had just received a large check from her insurance company for some water damage that had been caused by a leak in her roof. Then she said almost jubilantly: "So now Eric, I can finally buy the paints I need to fix up the house and when I am all done, I can put the house up for sale and move."

Eric asked her where she wanted to move to and she responded, "Probably to Hendersonville, North Carolina. I have been there several times and I really like it. I love the four seasons and the summers are so much cooler than in Florida."

"You know, Michelle," he said, "I hope you don't mind, but I have spoken to some of the guys at our men's club. I asked them if they would be willing to spend a Saturday helping to paint your house. They seemed very much in favor of doing so. Would you mind terribly if I pursue this further for you?"

"I really would not feel comfortable, Eric, to have a whole bunch of strange men walking around in my house. You and I could probably do the work ourselves. It would be fun working together and we would not have to worry about deadlines. Do you think you would like to help me sometimes?"

"I would like to Michelle," he said, "but I have very little experience in painting and decorating. I have never been very good with my hands. I admire people who are, but on occasion I have had problems even simply hammering a nail into a piece of wood. I probably have two left hands, so be forewarned."

Michelle squeezed his arm and told him that she was pretty good at this sort of thing and that she could show him all he needed to know.

By now, they had been walking for quite a long time and decided to sit on a bench to watch the wind and the sea put on their "Nature Play" as Michelle called it.

After a while, Eric suggested that before dropping her off at the Center to pick up her car, they could stop for a light meal. "Perhaps a salad would be perfect," he suggested. Eric loved salads. He had learned to like them when he had been so very ill and he contributed a great deal of his recovery to eating a properly balanced diet.

"Oh that is just what I am craving, Eric," she said. "There is a small little Italian restaurant just a short distance from here, on the other side of the bridge. Have you ever been there?"

"Do you know what it is called?" he asked.

"No," she said, "but I do know exactly where it is. I am sure I can find it."

They cleaned the sand from their shoes before getting into Eric's car and drove the short distance across the bridge. When they got to the top section of the rise, Eric looked to his left and admired the view. The sun was about to set and the wind was still whipping up the foamy waters of the Gulf. The view was spectacular. In the distance, he saw a single solitary sailboat returning and he could almost feel the exhilaration of her captain as he safely steered his small vessel back to port.

Michelle showed him where the small restaurant was. Eric had been there a few times and they decided to have their meal on the terrace.

The wind was now diminishing, the storm clouds had been swept clean from the skies and the moon was just beginning to show her chubby golden face, promises of a most pleasant evening.

They ate their meal without much talk, each of them absorbed in their own thoughts. Eric felt happy and relaxed. He hoped that this relationship would mature into the kind of togetherness that would make him happier than he had ever been before.

He asked her if she would like to go sailing the following Wednesday and they made a date to meet at eleven, with Eric promising to bring lunch.

Then, a little reluctantly, he drove her back to her car. Both of them occupied with their own thoughts, they talked little during the short trip there. Eric liked her silence. Sometimes people feel less of a need to talk when they intuitively sense a special connection.

He did not want to break up the enchanted spell of this

lovely evening and he felt sure that she was thinking the same, but he did not want to seem too forward, or too aggressive. He needed some time to be by himself, to reflect on what was happening to him. Was he proceeding too fast with this, he wondered. Was he allowing his emotions too much of a free range?

He lightly kissed her good-night and promised to pick her up the following Wednesday by eleven. He waited until she had started her car and then they both drove off in opposite directions.

When he came home, he sat on his pool-deck for a long time thinking about her. He realized he didn't know a great deal about her, but what he did know he liked very much.

He needed very much to talk to someone, rather than to keep council by himself. Perhaps it was just about getting confirmation that he was doing the right thing, but he didn't know who he could talk to. He never really developed the deep friendship which comes from knowing someone for a very long time. Someone you could totally trust and talk to. Besides, how would anyone know that this was right for him? "Go by what you feel in your guts Eric," he said out loud. "That what you honestly feel, can't be wrong. Even if it is, life is all about the things we still have to learn. Everything is in perfect order just the way it unfolds."

Finally he phoned Mary Beth. They had gone out a few times and he thought they had become friends. She was a very nice and intelligent woman, but there wasn't the chemistry for anything more between them and he had thought she understood that.

When he explained why he had phoned, she became quite upset and told him that he was cruel in talking to her about Michelle. She said, "When you get over your silly infatuation with her, call me and if I am still available we'll talk." With that she slammed down the phone.

Eric was quite shaken up by her behavior. "Silly woman," he thought to himself. All he had wanted to do was to express to her as a friend the confusion he felt. He had been wrong to trust her too much in this.

He went to the fridge and poured himself a glass of cool white wine and sat for a while longer while he sipped his wine pensively. He liked Mary Beth simply as a friend. What was he supposed to do now, stop liking her? What was it he had read in one of his many books on self improvement: Something about compassion and understanding and he remembered something about loving people unconditionally. He thought about the word "remember" and how if you would juxtapose it differently, like re-member, it meant to rejoin as a member. How that applied to Mary Beth, he did not know, but he did realize he had been wrong to call her a silly woman. "You were being judgmental Eric, your ego got in the way," and he was grateful then for having been given that insight.

Sleep would not come easily and he tossed and turned for a long time. Finally, he fell asleep but he had the strangest dream: He met the graceful and beautiful doe once more and again she looked deeply into his eyes. Her eyes were very large and big tears were dropping on the grass in front of her, making little puddles. This time she opened her narrow mouth to speak. Eric strained to hear what the message was but all he could hear was the rustling wind in the trees.

When he woke the next morning the sun had already started to brighten the horizon. I must hurry, he thought, if I want to jog on the golf course before the golfers arrive.

While he jogged, he thought about his dream and he decided to discard it as just a silly coincidence.

The deer were nowhere to be seen and after he showered, he decided to totally wipe his mind clean of everything that had happened and to just live his life each day as the best him he could be, to simply not worry about the future.

He picked her up at eleven sharp on Wednesday and he was pleasantly surprised to see that she was all ready. He liked that. Most of the women he had dated always kept him waiting for awhile. He didn't know if this was for special effects or if they really were not ready: "Let a guy know that you are not exactly waiting for him."

This was the first time he had seen her in shorts and he saw that her legs were elegantly slim. Her sandaled feet exposed bright red painted toenails and he admired her small feet. Her skin was soft and smooth, almost creamy white and he wondered how anyone living in Florida had managed to keep such a pale skin color.

On the way to his boat, they picked up some veggie wraps at the health food store and a few bottles of herbal tea.

Once on board, with their lunches now safely stowed in the icebox, he cast off expertly and they motored out under the bridge following the channel markers.

Once past the markers, he raised the sails and he was pleased to see that as he turned the boat windward causing Final Draft to heel substantially, she did not seem a bit nervous.

Michelle explained that her ex-husband had owned a small sailboat. This was when they had owned a beach house off Long Boat Key. She had done quite a lot of sailing then.

"I was married for fourteen years Eric, but we finally got a divorce, because Ted ran around a lot with other women and I couldn't stand it any longer. We had two adopted children: Maureen was eight at the time and Chuck was only four when we separated. I felt so horrible. We had adopted these two kids and then we wind up in divorce court.

"It was a real messy divorce too. Ted had taken precautions and had hidden much of his assets and I wound up with very little. It took years, and if my father hadn't helped out financially, I don't know how I could have managed. I became very depressed and as a result, Ted was awarded custody of the children. It was a very rough ride for me for many years. I could not work a lot because of my depressions but I was occasionally able to get short time temporary work just to help pay the bills.

"I was a teacher before all this happened, but I did not like teaching very much. I hated the system telling me all the time how to teach. Seven years ago I met Charlie and we were very happy for the first few years. After that, he often became angry and verbally abusive and my depressions began to return. So now, you know much of my whole life story Eric, how about telling me about yours?"

Eric explained about his illness and his divorce from Jane and her unexpected departure back to Toronto. He told her that he missed Jamie very much but that there had been very little he could have done about Jane leaving Florida. He had given her custody, trusting her and not ever imagining that she would do this to him.

This was all too much negative talk, Eric decided and if they would go on this way, it would surely spoil their afternoon sail.

The winds were almost too perfect, with not too much of a heel. Final Draft was handling beautifully, doing about five knots he guessed and they ate their lunch on deck while the boat was in Auto Helm.

In order to change the subject and to steer their conversation onto a different more positive topic, Eric quite innocently said, "Can you tell me something Michelle? If you only had a short time left on this earth, what would you want to do more than anything else in this world?"

She did not hesitate when she replied, "Go to a cabin in the mountains of Northern Georgia in the fall. I have always wanted to do this. To be close to nature and go for long walks in the woods is what I would really want to do if I ever was given a choice."

Eric was a bit surprised by what she had said to him but he countered, "Well, why don't we do this then. I will go on the internet and find us a nice cabin in the woods where we can stay for a week or so. The leaves are changing and it should be beautiful this time of the year. Why don't you give this some serious thought Michelle? We should be allowed to do those things that we most enjoy doing."

"Are you telling me you would be willing to do this for me?"

"Of course I would," Eric replied without hesitating. "Although I have never been in the Georgia mountains, I am sure I would enjoy it as much as you would, especially this time of the year. You just think about it some more and in the meantime I will search the internet and see what is available."

By now it was getting late. It was time to head Final Draft back to port. He figured it would take them at least two hours to sail back in and then an hour or so to tie her down and tidy her up. He did not like to come in when it was too dark. It would make his job of tying her down much more difficult.

It was almost six by the time he had finished all that

needed to be done before he could leave the boat securely tied up. By now, they were both quite tired from their long day out in the sun and the wind.

He drove her home, kissed her gently and said that he would phone her in a few days to get her reply regarding their trip to Georgia.

When he went on the Net the following day, Eric did find exactly what sounded like just the place they would both enjoy. It had two bedrooms. He had not discussed this part with her but he was positive that she would be more comfortable having her own privacy. He thought it wise, that at this point of their relationship, neither one of them would want to rush things.

He printed out the advertisement because he thought that she might like to see it. The place was set off the beaten track, deep in the woods. It had a nicely appointed kitchen and a fireplace. The hottub as well as the barbeque were located on a large wrap-around veranda. It was letter perfect, he thought.

When he called a few days later, her machine was on again and he left a message for her to call him back.

She returned his call later that week and he described the place he had found. "Michelle," he said, "I know we did not discuss this, but I think you would feel more comfortable if you had the privacy of your own bedroom. I think this would be more in integrity for both of us."

"I think that you are very gracious in suggesting this Eric," she said. "I know we are going to have a wonderful time. I spoke to my spiritual director about going and she thought this could be very good for me. So yes, I would be delighted to accept your invitation. But Eric, I do not have the money to contribute to the cost. Are you okay with this?"

"Of course I am. Perhaps we could drive. This would defray the flight cost and we could make it a real little vacation by stopping over for the first night in Jacksonville Beach and then drive from there to Savannah, where we could overnight for the second night. From there it would not be terribly far to drive the rest of the way. Why don't we leave in a few days? I will phone tomorrow to see what they have available."

They departed the following Friday. She drove over to his house and parked her car in his garage.

Eric had wondered why she wanted to consult with her spiritual director and he had intended to ask her about this later during their drive up.

On the trip over to Jacksonville she talked a bit about her family and he asked her if she had told her parents that she was going away. Again Eric was a little surprised when she told him that she had told no one else.

He wondered about this with some concerns, but then, he shrugged it off like so many other times, when over the next several months, he discovered things about her somewhat strange behavior.

He concluded that she was very different from him. But was that so wrong? Surely his perceptions about things were bound to be different from hers.

Chapter
FIVE

Eric was beginning to get mixed signals.

It was early evening. They had used the afternoon of their arrival checking out the place and orientating themselves. Then, they went for a long walk along some of the many trails. The weather was a lot cooler up here in the mountains in Northern Georgia and they changed into sweaters and of course their hiking boots. Eric's were almost a brand new pair. He had bought them at Nordstrom's in Colorado when he had been up there the previous summer. He'd done a little hiking in the mountains then, but his boots were not yet fully broken in.

They went grocery shopping in the little village at Wal-Mart and Michelle had remarked how pleasant and friendly people were here as compared to in Florida. Eric didn't think so. He had found that people in Florida were usually very nice. He thought that it might have something to do with the climate and the sunshine. "But," he explained, "In comparison, people in small towns were bound to be a little different."

He had done the cooking that evening and Michelle had helped as his Sous Chef, assisting him with much of the preparation and the cleaning up. She seemed to have no problem fitting into this role and Eric had always enjoyed doing the creative part of the cooking. He disliked the cleaning up afterwards.

He usually did not use cookbooks. He just sort of knew intuitively what went well together. He was one of those individuals who could almost tell how things would taste before he flavored the food and he always knew precisely which spices and how much of them he should use.

Michelle had been much impressed with his culinary art and her compliments made him feel like someone had just pinned the Congressional Medal of Honor on him.

The dishes had been washed and put away and he liked how quick and efficiently she did things.

Now, they played with the radio dials until they found a station which played soft classical music. They lit the fireplace, sat down on the overstuffed couch, put their stocking feet on the little coffee table in front of them, finished their glass of wine and talked of the past few days.

"I have really loved our time together Eric," Michelle said. "I enjoyed Jacksonville Beach, I think Savannah is a very interesting town and today was such a perfectly beautiful day for our drive up here. I listened carefully to what you told me about yourself and I know we share much the same philosophies."

"I believe we can become very good friends. What do you think Eric, of having close women friends even if those relationships never become more than just friendships?"

"I am a little confused by what I am hearing you say," Eric responded. "Of course I would like to be friends Michelle, but I also feel that it could easily become much more than that. At least I am hoping that it will. Should I rein in those feelings and not let this happen? Do you not also think that you could fall in love with me or develop stronger feelings for me?"

"I don't want to hurt your feelings Eric, but I really think you are little too old for me. You are seventeen years my senior and I am concerned that this could become too much of a difference. Besides, I don't feel a physical attraction for you. Not in that way. I do like you very much, please don't take this the wrong way, but I don't really think that the chemistry is there for us to become lovers."

Eric felt quite devastated by what she had just said. Why this was so he could not really understand. After all, she had only been very honest with him. It was not meant as a rejection, so why did he have such negative feelings about what she had just shared? He instantly became withdrawn and he could actually feel his mood changing from that wonderful exhilaration of the rush one feels when one starts to fall in love, into a dull and defeated hopelessness.

How could she make him think one moment that their relationship could mature into something more, something he had been searching for most of his adult life, only to so cruelly let him down the next instant? What kind of a person would do this?

But then he realized that she hadn't actually ever encouraged him to feel this way. Certainly not by what she had said or how she had acted. This was his own thinking, his own hoping, his own doing and he now began to understand about his lifelong failure to see things in light of the present moment, without his silly dreams for the future. The future, he finally realized, would take care of itself. It hadn't happened yet and he should not try to manipulate or control it. He began to understand that his thoughts had led him into this thinking and that he had inadvertently created an environment where his wrong perceptions controlled his emotional well being.

Despondently, he decided to go to bed. He said goodnight to her and he retired to his bedroom.

He would not be able to sleep of course, he knew that and unless he used the meditation tapes which he had brought with him, he would be up for most of the night fretting about this. God, he hated himself for feeling this way!

Meditating always seemed to make him feel better. He'd become more relaxed and feel at peace. It helped him to chase away all of those thoughts which he intuitively realized, did not serve him well.

After listening to the tapes for an hour he felt better and he fell asleep almost instantly.

He dreamed of the doe again. This time, he was in a dense forest and Michelle was there with him. The doe looked at them very sadly with her large brown eyes and he noticed there was something very different about her head. Something he was sure, he had not noticed before. He looked closer and now he was sure: there were two large horns protruding from her head.

When he woke, earlier than he had intended, he thought about his dream for a long time, but he couldn't figure out what it meant.

He quietly got up and went for an early morning walk. It was quite foggy, but the forest was lovely and in a somber sort of way, it reflected his mood perfectly. Everything was dripping wet and he could clearly hear the ticking sound all around him of a multitude of falling drops on the moist damp earth and on the rapidly yellowing leaves. The smell was musty fragrant, like the scent of decaying leaves and fallen tree trunks which were evident in abundance everywhere and whose shapes played tricks on his imagination in the dim light of this early morning hour.

The beginning of another day, Eric thought, and perhaps today, Michelle might be able to look at him in a different light.

It was important, he thought, that he continue to look at things objectively. There wasn't anything wrong with him and there really was no reason that he could think of for her not to be physically attracted to him.

Yes, he was seventeen years older than she was, but no one could tell. Many people who met him for the first time, thought that he was in his late fifties or early sixties. He was a pretty good looking guy, in fact many of his friends thought he looked amazingly like Richard Gere.

He was a man of substantial means and if she didn't want him, then that was simply her misfortune. There were lots of other women who would be interested in him, he thought and in Florida there was no shortage of nice looking single women.

When he retuned to the cabin, she greeted him and smiled her wonderful bright flashing smile. "You better take off those wet things, Eric and take a nice hot shower. I will have breakfast ready when you are done. Or maybe you might like to soak for a while in the hottub. I lifted the cover earlier and the water is nice and hot. I am sure you would enjoy it."

He decided to take a shower and said, "The hottub sounds inviting, but perhaps we can save that experience for later in the evening when we can both do some star gazing."

He liked the way she made his breakfast. The bacon done in the microwave, wasn't greasy and his toast and eggs where just right. Making great tasting coffee however wasn't her forte because she so seldom had it for breakfast, and he decided that in the future he should probably make it himself.

"In the future," he thought. "Will there be a future in their relationship?" But then he immediately dropped the thought and instead decided to simply concentrate on the here and now and just enjoy their present moments together. "God Almighty Eric," he thought, "you are just too much. Just stop worrying and relax. Not everything needs to go according to your idea of a grandiose and well defined plan. Just enjoy your life the way it comes."

The weather cleared and they spent the rest of the day having a wonderful time going for long walks along some of the many trails in the area.

They discovered a little grassy plot of land surrounded by a small lake with a little wooden bridge connecting it to the mainland and they laid down in the sweet smelling grass sunning themselves in the warm and pleasant sunshine of this beautiful early fall day.

Michelle had to be very careful. Her skin was creamy white and quite sensitive to the sun. She had covered her head with her sweater and she promptly fell asleep. Eric decided to walk back across the little bridge and to take a picture of her sleeping.

She was sprawled out there, like an innocent little girl and the only thing which took away from this portrait of her perfect harmony with nature, was the sweater covering her head. Later, back in the cabin, when he showed her the picture by plugging his camera into the T.V., he had entitled it: "Sleeping Headless Beauty in Georgia." He promised to print it out for her on his computer after they returned home.

The cabin they had rented included access to additional recreational facilities. There was a sizable community clubhouse available to them as part of their package. Here, they discovered a billiard table, a separate little kitchen and a stereo system with a small dance floor.

Eric had never been very good at playing billiards, in fact he didn't much care for the game. Michelle explained that she had played it a lot with her dad when she was younger and she said, "I bet I can beat you Eric. Let's play a game and you can name your price in case you win."

He replied, "I can't possibly imagine what I could ask for in case I win. I don't want us to play for money." Then he said smirking, "I could ask you to slowly undress in front of me and then to make passionate love to me."

"That's two things Eric. Gosh, you are a greedy person. Of course you could always ask, but it doesn't mean that you would get it," she replied jokingly.

Eric let out a sigh of mock relief and said, "Thank God, for a brief moment there I was under the impression that you wanted me so passionately that you would secretly let me win."

Her laugh was warm and sincere and her smile had that brilliance that he had come to admire.

"Now Eric," she giggled, "you are really being naughty. You would have to win first in any case before you could ask for such a price and that will never happen in a million years."

They played their first game and although he tried very hard and put in his utmost best effort, he lost pitifully. He immediately demanded another game, insisting on the same stake and then another but she won each time. Finally, with her feeling very victorious and him letting her graciously enjoy her victories, they walked back to the cabin, arm in arm.

It was a cool night. The temperature must have been close to freezing, but wearing their warm heavy woolen sweaters, they did not seem to feel the chill in the night air. Out there above the woods, the heavens were filled with stars. They looked up and admired the night vista and a splendid full moon which illuminated the otherwise obscure path back to their cabin.

She squeezed his arm tenderly and said, "Eric I am having such a great time. Thank you so very much for bringing me out here."

He didn't think that a response was required. He didn't know what to say. The squeeze on his arm seemed innocent enough but it dared to give him a tiny little bit of hope.

When they arrived back at the cabin, before going inside, they both removed their boots and left them neatly outside on the porch. They lit the fireplace and then Eric suggested that they change into their bathing suits and get into the hottub.

Their skin tingling from the cold air, and giggling like young kids, they ran the short distance across the veranda to where the hottub was located. Hurriedly they removed the cover and got into the jet-agitated pleasantly hot water. The smell of chlorine was a bit overwhelming, but they accepted this minor discomfort when they looked up into the heavens and saw the spectacle and the brilliance of a thousand stars.

They talked of their dreams and their aspirations. They spoke of their lives and what they would change if they could do it all over again.

After a while, they became so relaxed that even talking

became a chore and they decided that it was time to take showers and go to bed.

He lightly kissed her goodnight, being very careful not to make it appear as passionate as he felt, but he was almost sure that she held him a little bit closer than she had done previously. He was convinced that it was not his imagination working overtime and that night he slept, feeling hopeful once again.

This time, when he woke, there was no fog and the day gave promise of much sunshine and of brilliant clear blue skies. Through the dazzling golden rays of sunshine, cascaded down the tree foliage, Eric could see clearly how the light breezes assisted nature in the downward floating and spiraling of a multitudes of gold and red leaves, being carried once again to their yearly resting place. The view through their large kitchen windows was spectacular.

Michelle apparently had been awake for some time as well, because when he quietly rummaged around in the bathroom, she came out of her bedroom and they decided to enjoy this beautiful morning by going for a nice long walk before having breakfast.

Eric was on the porch first and he couldn't find one of his boots. He called out to her, "Hey Michelle, what tricks do I have to perform for you in return for one of my boots?"

She came out on the porch almost immediately and said, "Eric I did not hide your boot, honestly, I did not."

"Sure, sure," he answered, and it sounded perhaps a bit more impatient than he had intended. "You had your fun. Now please tell me where it is. I don't relish the thought of having to hobble around on one foot for the rest of the day."

They looked on the ground below the steps to see if one of the boots might have fallen off the porch. Last night, before leaving, they had neglected to leave a light on the porch and in the dark it seemed entirely possible that he had placed one boot too close to the edge. After a while, they had to admit that the missing boot was nowhere to be found and they wondered why someone would steal one boot and not take them both.

Eric went to get his running shoes and they decided that after their walk and after breakfast, they would check with Bill, the owner of the cabins, who ran the small resort. Perhaps he might have an explanation for this strange occurrence.

They walked for a long time, enjoying the clear fresh morning air, the crunching of a thick blanket of dry leaves under their feet and the pleasure of each other's company.

They laid down on a large fallen tree trunk, head to head, looking up at the clear blue skies through a myriad of foliage while enveloping themselves in the rapidly warming sunshine.

On the way back to their cabin, they met up with Bill and when Eric explained what had happened, Bill burst out laughing even before he had a chance to finish telling him the complete story of the strange disappearance of one of his boots.

Bill explained that one of his neighbors had a little brown and black dog which had developed a strange habit of playfully stealing a single boot from porches. The dog would playfully carry it to a place in the woods and later, he would usually return it near or close to the place from where he had first taken it.

At first they thought that Bill was joking but after they came back to their cabin, indeed Eric's missing boot was found just on the other side of the porch.

Eric was glad of course to have his boot back. They were now well broken in and they promised each other that this was one story they would not likely ever forget.

The balance of the time went by much too quick. They danced at night in the little clubhouse, cooked great meals together in their small kitchen and they even played some more pool. Eric did manage to win one game. It was on the final night of their stay and he immediately demanded the spoils of his win, but Michelle laughingly said, "Eric, that was then, and this is now. The rules are not the same, because you now have a little more experience and so you can not have the same prize."

In the end, he received his prize, a far greater one than he had dared to hope for.

It came about very natural. He had massaged her small and elegant feet. She had complimented him on how well he had done this. "Where did you learn to do this so well?" she asked. They were sitting on the couch in front of the fireplace and he kissed her quite spontaneously. She had returned his kiss more passionately than he had ever been kissed before.

Eric had not had sex for quite some time. It was not that he did not have a number of opportunities, but ever since the severe radiation treatments, he had been afraid, because he had read somewhere that becoming sexually active, could again feed the cancer.

He was surprised when he could not have a strong enough erection to even enter her. They were both disappointed of course and now Eric was concerned not only because he felt less as a man, but also, he was worried how Michelle would feel about this. She had become so much more responsive to him in these last few days and he had hoped that in time, she would come to love him.

He thought about that first night when she had told him that he was not appealing to her, what was it she had said? Oh yes, "That the chemistry was missing and that there was too much of difference in their ages."

Now he wondered, what had brought about this change in her thinking and how his lack of being able to have a satisfactory erection would affect her thinking? And then he thought: She has become so very different from when they had first met and when he had felt so very sorry for her. She had changed from what had appeared to him then, to be such a helpless person who had seemed to almost beg to be loved, into a personality which was quite confident and very wonderful to be with.

They talked very little on the drive back to Clearwater the next day and he had quite convinced himself that after she had collected her car at his place, he would probably never see her again.

But she surprised him once more. When they were an hour or so away from his home she said, "Eric, thank you so very much for a lovely time. I don't really want to go back to my house. I don't like it there anymore. It has the wrong energy for me. I am not sure if you can understand this? I am now in a good and very positive frame of mind and I would like to keep it this way. Would you mind very much if I stayed with you for a while?"

Eric searched her face very closely. He was shocked. He could not believe what he had just heard. This was such a wonderful surprise! He said, "Michelle, but of course you can honey, stay as long as you like."

"Thank you Eric, but please don't call me 'Honey.' I hate that. I am not your 'Honey.'"

Chapter
SIX

During the first few days after their return, Michelle had asked Eric if he was okay with her moving some of her things into the spare bedroom. "I would like to feel that I can have a space where I have some privacy," she had said.

Eric fully recognized her need for privacy, in fact he welcomed her suggestion and said, "Michelle, you are my guest and of course I want you to feel comfortable for as long as you remain here. When were you thinking of going back to your own house?"

"I haven't really thought about it much Eric, I feel very comfortable being here. Your place is so much brighter and more comfortable than mine. I really feel very much at peace. We could go back to my house occasionally to do some painting and to decorate the place a little, so I can sell it more easily."

Eric couldn't quite understand why she preferred to remain with him, rather than going back to her own place. Her house was not as comfortable as his, that part was true, but he thought it was certainly quite adequate. He did not think however, that this was an important issue to worry about and he decided not to question her any further.

Privately, he shrugged his shoulders and thought: "I think I am in love with her. This may be a good way for me to get to know her better and to become more sure of how I feel. Perhaps Michelle feels the same way as I do, but at this point, she may not want to talk about it and this might well be one of her reasons for her wanting to remain at my house. When she is ready to talk about it, she will."

But she continued to spend her nights in his spare bedroom. They had not slept together since that last night in the cabin in Northern Georgia.

A few days later, after they spend most of the day at her house painting, she said to Eric, "I am sure that your muscles must be as sore as mine. When we get to your house, could we please take a hot bath together in your large whirlpool? Then after, I will give you a good massage. You certainly deserve a little spoiling after all the work you did. And if you promise to behave yourself, I will let you do the same for me." She flashed her wonderful smile, which always disarmed him.

Later that evening she decided to sleep in his bed and the following day, she moved her things down to his bedroom.

They made love and this time, much to his relief, he was able to have an erection. He struggled to hold off his orgasm as long as he could but it seemed to him that it took her a very long time to be ready and he finally had to let go.

He lay there, gasping for a while until his breathing became more regular.

She was disappointed, he could tell.

She said, "I am really frustrated Eric. I needed this release as much as you did. Couldn't you have held off just a little longer?"

He didn't want to tell her that he had tried as best he

could, instead, he apologized, and for the second time in their love making history, he felt less than the man he had once been before he had become ill.

"Honey, it does not always happen that couples have orgasms at the same time. It would be wonderful if we could learn to make this so, but there will be times that you will have one and I will not. Please understand that I feel very fortunate to have an orgasm at all, after all the radiation I've had. I know I care about you enough to be delighted whenever I can please you, without necessarily having to please myself and I would not resent it in the least, whenever I am able to give you these gifts. You can return these to me at other times and in so many different ways. For this is how I see it: Giving each other our gifts of love."

Surprisingly, she did not respond directly to what he had said. Instead, she said, "Eric, would you please not call me 'your honey.' You say this to all the waitresses in the restaurants and I do not like it when you call me that."

They talked for a while longer and then, she picked up one of her favorite books on self improvement and began to read. Eric did not remember how long she read. He was exhausted and was asleep almost at the very instant when he turned to his sleeping side.

Thanksgiving came and went. They had gone to her parents for the usual turkey fixings and Eric met some of her family. He played on their badly tuned baby-grand and they were all very impressed with his musical talents.

Michelle's mother was so pleased that her daughter had finally found a nice suitor, she kept bringing him more chocolate cookies while her dad kept himself occupied by refilling Eric's wine glass, both of which he politely refused. He was concerned that the wine might loosen his tongue too much and he wanted to be careful about what he said that first time he met her family.

Michelle had told him some time ago that they were "good Christians." Eric did not know exactly what that meant. It sounded strange to him and he couldn't decide if this term offended him or not. He figured you were either a good person or a bad person, religion did not enter into it. He wondered if they knew that he was Jewish and if so, would they label him as a good or a bad Jew?

The day after Thanksgiving, his sister called.

"Eric," Sybille had said, "Raymond and I are flying out to Nassau next week for a few days. Would you and Michelle like to join us there? We are staying at the British Colonial. Why don't you call your travel agent and see what kind of reservations you can get and then call us back."

Eric thought that this would be a nice way for Michelle to meet his sister and brother-in-law; but he also thought that Sybille might have an ulterior motive. Was she being overly protective and wanted to see with her own eyes what he had described to them as "the woman of my dreams."

He knew his sister well enough. He had been married twice before, and this time he thought she wanted to make sure that he went into this relationship with both of his eyes wide open. She had always thought that Eric was an incurable romantic, and she was probably right.

He was not at all sure that Sybille trusted this latest flame of his. Oh well, he thought, once they meet her, they will surely change their minds. They will be suitably impressed. Of that he was sure.

They met them on the small private beach behind the British Colonial. As Eric made the introductions, he watched his sister closely. She had a habit of squinting her eyes a little, whenever she was alarmed about something or other. It was imperceptible to most people, but if you knew what to look for, you could easily spot it.

And there it was! So, he had been right after all, he thought. It doesn't matter. After they get to know Michelle, they will love her as much as he did.

Time went by far too quickly. They dined, shopped, danced and of course did a lot of swimming in the crystal clear waters of the Bahamas. After five short days, they were back home again and Nassau became another memory in their book of memories which they had so lovingly started to write in a mountain cabin in Northern Georgia.

Michelle said she loved to dance and Eric had arranged to take dancing lessons. He could move reasonably well on a crowded dance floor, but ballroom dancing was quite another thing.

On their first lessons he became aware of something that he found contradictory to all of her previous behaviors. She would consistently remind him to lead her more firmly and to apply some pressure on her shoulder blades in order to let her know what his intentions were. He thought, "She wants me to be more forceful and show her who is leading who."

She explained, "Dancing is all about communication Eric, and unless you communicate well with your partner, it isn't going to work."

He thought, "She is not only just referring to dancing is she?" He good-naturedly tried to do better at leading her but every once in a while she wasn't able to pass up the opportunity of reminding him of his missed responsibilities.

Michelle had approached him about taking a weekend seminar of Imago training. She had shown him some videos of how couples could benefit and discover how to improve their communication skills with each other. Eric thought that this was a wonderful idea, especially since they were just starting out as a couple. He was convinced that this could help them both improve their collective skills and he enrolled them for a weekend in early December.

During the Sunday morning session she admitted to the class that it was difficult for her to commit fully to their relationship because she never had proper closure to her previous relationship with Charlie, the man Eric had met at the Center.

During the lunch break he told Michelle that her admission had been very upsetting to him. This was completely out of left field, he said and he couldn't understand why she had never shared this with him before he had enrolled them in this seminar. He said, "Michelle, it isn't right for us to be in this relationship if you have not yet had closure from the previous one. I do not want to break off our relationship, but I do want you to meet with Charlie and decide once and for all, if it is over. If it is not, I believe it would be better for us not to see each other again." He insisted that she call and arrange to meet him.

She made an appointment to meet with Charlie the following Saturday, early in the afternoon, and before she left, Eric asked, "Michelle, will you be here for dinner?" She responded, "I do not expect that we are going to be longer than a few hours. We are meeting on Sand Key Beach. If I am going to be late, I will call."

But she hadn't called and she finally returned close to nine that evening.

Eric was very upset about this, but he decided to control his anger. He was beginning to understand that he could never change her thoughtlessness. If he loved her and if he wanted to continue their relationship, he had better try to change his ways of processing all that went on in his own mind.

That Saturday afternoon and the early evening had been terribly difficult for him and time passed agonizingly slow. Eric had always been a man of action and during this long waiting period of inactivity, he of course imagined all kinds of scenarios.

Most of his thoughts were about blaming himself for having been such an ass to ask her to meet with her previous lover. For all he knew, they were probably making love while he was waiting, with their cold dinner, for the verdict. He knew he was not able to compete with a healthy man after what they had done to his body during the lengthy radiation. Some weeks ago, she had made a point to let him know that she and Charlie had great sex very often.

Yes, he had been cancer free for several years now, he thought but there had been a price to pay.

When she finally returned, she did not volunteer any explanation as to why she was so terribly late. No apologies either.

He asked her how things went.

"It went very well Eric," she explained. "We talked for a long time and he does not want to re-enter into our previous relationship."

So that was that, he thought! And he let out an inaudible sigh of relief.

She went on and said, "I appreciated his candor and now I guess I have to become realistic and recognize that what we once had, we could never recapture. So it is now officially over between us. I guess that's what you wanted to hear, isn't it Eric?" He didn't know if she was just very unhappy or if she was being sarcastic.

He did not respond, but later that evening, he thought about their conversation for a long time and he could not figure out why she had started with their relationship when she so obviously still was in love with Charlie.

What was it then, that she had felt for him? She could not possible have been in love with both of them, or could she? He felt like he had just become her booby prize. He also thought that she had used him as an alternative, perhaps because of how well he could provide for her. He would have far preferred it if she had chosen him because of the kind of person he was. This, he thought, wasn't love. It was what one would call "trading." Love, he thought, wasn't something with a price tag on it. It was something you gave freely, without any strings attached, without any conditions.

Christmas and New Years came and went and Sybille had called to tell him about a townhouse she had found a little north of Toronto which had a balcony overlooking a protected forest area.

Eric, for some time now had been thinking about how he could spend more quality time with Jamie.

After the divorce, when Jane and Jamie had moved back to Toronto, he had tried to fly up there every month or so.

On those weekends, he would have dinner with Jamie and occasionally they would even catch a movie together, but Eric thought that the strong bonding they had once both enjoyed when they had lived together as a family in Florida, was quickly beginning to disappear.

He didn't like that, and he couldn't think of a way to fix it, other than by buying a place of his own in Toronto and by dividing his time between his two homes. He hoped that in this way, they would once again become closer, but when he expressed his concerns to Michelle, she told him not to expect too much.

She explained, "She is a teenager now Eric. There are all kinds of things happening to her young body at her age. Just don't expect too much too soon."

Then too, they had talked about her plans. She had not as yet put her house up for sale. He noticed that it usually took her a lot longer to make decisions.

Early in January, Eric told her, "I am flying up to Toronto in a few weeks. Would you like to come along Michelle? I know at this time you are not seriously considering moving there with me, but you might like it up there, and this would get you out of Florida for those hot summers that you so despise. I plan to at least spend the summer months there. It would give you an opportunity to see the place that Sybille has raved so much about."

They saw the townhouse and instantly fell in love with it. There was a small living room and dining room, a good size kitchen with a combination kitchen/eating area and family room, which was divided in the center by a gas fireplace. From there, French double doors led to a balcony which overlooked a small birch forest.

Eric decided this time not to act in haste, the way he usually did. He spoke to the agent before returning to Florida and arranged with him, to put in an offer by fax, in the event that he decided to buy the place.

Six weeks later, after his offer had been accepted he decided to fly back to Toronto again. This time, to pick the color schemes and he invited Michelle to come along again.

"You do have such very good taste and you seem to have a flair for colors," he told her and they spent several days going over tile samples, selecting wall colors and picking out fixtures and appliances.

The legal transfer and taking of possession of the new townhouse was arranged to take place by the end of April and Eric decided to go up to Toronto one last time to check on the progress.

This time, he did not ask Michelle to come along with him. Firstly, there was little point in doing so and then too, he wanted her to take the necessary time to make a decision on her own, should she want to move with him. He knew it was at times difficult for her to make decisions, and it would be good to have some time to herself to reflect on that.

"While I am away," he said, when she drove him to the airport, "you will have lots of time to think about what you want to do."

Eric's house had been sold and the new owners were due to take possession in June. He had contracted for a moving company to move his things to the new townhouse and he figured that in the event that Michelle should decide to move with him, they could always include the things from her house that she would want to take.

He was pleasantly surprised on his return, when she picked him up at the airport and after she passionately embraced him, she said, "Eric I have thought about this very carefully, in fact I have thought of little else. I have decided that I would like to move with you and that I would like to get married here in Florida before we leave."

Eric was elated with this news of course, although he could not understand what had brought about this shift in her thinking. He should have asked her then, but he did not. He thought the timing was all wrong and he would have lots of opportunity to ask her later. Even if he had asked her, she in all probability would not have been able to give him a reasonable explanation, although being in love with him, he thought, would have been enough of a valid reason.

Much later, when he thought about this, he realized that this should have been a warning for him, but would he have heeded it? Why had he not listened to his inner voice? After his illness had he not yet learned to become more conscious of this? Who was he, to argue with that which had taught him so much about himself since his recovery?

On the drive back to his house, they both became caught up in the excitement of their future together as a couple and they talked eagerly and endlessly about their wedding plans.

There was not a whole lot of time, they both realized. It was already the end of March, and there were many things to do if they planned to depart for Toronto towards the end of April.

He had explained to her that he would insist on them signing a prenuptial agreement before their marriage. He said, "I know one most important ingredient in a marriage is trust and if we were both starting out as youngsters in this adventure of our lives together, there would not be a need for a prenuptial." He stopped and reflected briefly because he wanted to get this next part right.

"I really do believe in the principals Michelle, that when a young couple gets married and they work together to build up their assets, in the event that their marriage should fail, they own these assets jointly, because they have earned it together.

"But this is very different. I have considerable assets and you have very little. In the event that our marriage should fail, it is only fair that we each get to keep what we start out with."

She did not answer but he was beginning to understand a little better how her mind worked and he knew that she had to think this through.

In the end they did sign the agreement he had wanted, but she insisted that their new home in Toronto be jointly owned and Eric did not think that this was an unreasonable request, considering that she was moving to a new country where she did not know a soul. He wanted at any rate for her to have this security in the event something was to happen to him. Later of course, when things began to go wrong, he thought that he should have added some sort of a time element in this clause, but by then it was too late and his lawyer had failed to advise him on this issue.

Eric had already begun to pack some of his things in boxes before he had left on his latest trip to Toronto, but now, there were also all of her things to sort through and pack.

He prided himself on being an organized person, and he sometimes had difficulties handling last minute changes in his plans. As a result, whenever this happened, the pressures made him behave in ways he disliked in himself.

"Eric," he counseled himself one morning, "if you don't like the way you act, then you need to change the conditions which make you behave this way, or you need to change your reactive behavior. You and you alone have the power to change this."

They set their wedding date for April the 6th. Michelle wanted to have a garden wedding and together they looked at a large variety of options. The Wedding Gardens, near Indian Rocks Beach, where Michelle had done some volunteer work, and she therefore knew some of the people in charge, was one place they both seem to favor.

Eric had to admit that it was indeed a lovely setting. There were various different types of garden arrangements to choose from. The rose garden, with a beautiful heart-shaped trellis covered with large bright red and pink aromatic roses, was particularly attractive. Many of these settings were specially made for small wedding parties like theirs. Some even had heart-shaped benches with small water fountains in the background.

They both loved the gardens and any one of these would have made an outstanding choice, but because of the extremely short time left till their wedding date, they were unable to book it for the 6th.

Finally, after much deliberation they decided to have their wedding at Eric's house. His house had a lovely garden overlooking a small lake and the setting was perfectly beautiful with large trees overhanging the water's edge.

They wondered why they hadn't thought of it before. "You know Michelle," Eric said after they had decided, "sometimes we overcomplicate our life to the point where we fail to see the obvious."

Michelle shopped for days on end looking for just the right outfits. She spent a lot more money than she had intended. Eric had always thought that she had a somewhat frugal personality trait and he was surprised at the enormous mountain of clothing she had modeled for him one night late, after she returned home, very excited about all her purchases.

Sometimes they argued about her staying out many hours past the time when she had promised to be back.

Eric thought it strange when she knew she was going to be so much later, that she wouldn't take a minute to phone him to let him know that she was alright.

Michelle responded with, "Look Eric, it isn't always con-

venient for me to find a phone. I can take care of myself and
I am a very good driver, so stop worrying all the time when
I am a little late."

A little late was sometimes three or four hours and Eric
thought, "She just doesn't seem to get it. It is a matter of consideration and respect, yes of even loving your partner to be
considerate enough to pick up a phone to let him know that
you are going to be late for supper."

When he knew she was going to be late coming back, he
would cook their supper. He didn't mind that, he liked to
cook for her and he always felt good when she complimented him on his culinary art.

He was mostly concerned with her thoughtlessness, but
he thought, "She probably doesn't do this consciously," and
he wrote her lack of consideration off on the fact that the
wedding was so close at hand and that they had yet so many
things to do. Deep down though, something was bothering
him about this and he wondered about this idiosyncrasy in
her personality.

The wedding almost became a disaster when first
Michelle was late and then her daughter was even later, while
his good friend Nora, their minister, told him that if his bride
did not get there soon, she would have to leave, since she had
another function to attend to.

Again he pondered silently what kind of a person he was
marrying. After all, they had not known each other very
long. But then he thought, "It really does not matter how
long you know a person. Do you ever actually get to know
someone well, even if you have been together for a long
time?" He and Jane had known each other for well over thirteen years and how much of a difference had this made?

Then, he made a conscious effort of pushing these

thoughts out of his mind. "You are just having a case of pre-marital jitters," he thought.

On the Sunday following their wedding, he had booked a suite at the Don Cesar Hotel. He wanted so much to please her and he knew that being on the beach and going for long walks along the Gulf was something they both liked to do and that this would make her happy. They couldn't stay long of course, because there was so much to do before the move, but at least it was a short weekend get-away for both of them to celebrate their marriage.

The remaining weeks went by very quickly and Eric was too preoccupied to notice some of her strange behaviors which seemed to be so out of character for her. Perhaps he had not wanted to notice them and he thought: "Once we are settled in our new home in Toronto, I can help her work on these issues." He concluded that possibly these might still be the remnants of the depressions she had been suffering when they had first met.

It was very late at night, when they finally drove away, leaving his barren and empty house behind. The moving van had only just left and he had walked through the rooms of his house one final last time to say his goodbye. These rooms in his house, were now so very devoid of any personality, that special flavor which he had added to them, while he had lived there.

He didn't know whether to be happy or sad, but he did feel an emptiness somewhere in his chest cavity. There were lots of memories buried here and he remembered again the hurt and pain he had felt when he first found out that Jane and Jamie were leaving. Then, he shrugged, locked the door behind him and forced himself not to look back as he backed out of the driveway.

It was close to midnight. The moving van had come much later than expected. They were both drained from the long day and had decided to try to drive a little northbound, before checking into a motel for the night.

They drove her car. He had left his Volvo convertible with Michelle's dad until they returned in early June, after the closing, when the new owners would take possession of his house. They would then drive his car north and he had promised Michelle that they might try to make a little mini vacation out of the drive.

Her car was the kind where you could fold back the rear seats, so they could accommodate more of their personal belongings. They would need these, since the van line would not deliver their things for at least ten days after their arrival in Toronto and his Volvo just did not have very much trunk space.

They were both exhausted and after two hours of driving they pulled into a Holiday Inn and slept.

Eric dreamed the fuzzy-warm dreams about his marriage and his bride, both of which promised to finally bring him the happiness he had longed for, so very much for so long.

Two days of driving northbound to their destination did not bring him that promise, and the wonderful feelings he should ordinarily have experienced from the exciting prospect of starting a new life together in a new place and in a new home were absent.

Michelle became more and more contrary and argumentative. Almost arrogant, he thought. Eric took most of her sometimes vicious remarks good-naturedly.

He thought he knew why she acted that way. "What would it be like for me," he thought, "if I were moving to a new country where I knew very few people, with a partner that I didn't really know all that well either? Of course she is scared and feels insecure. All she needs now is lots of loving kindness and understanding."

The day after their arrival, Eric paid a visit to the lawyer who would close the deal and would arrange to have the townhouse registered in both their names.

A small voice deep inside of him tried to caution him, but Eric had agreed on the terms of the prenuptial and although it would have been relatively easy for him not to have the registration done in both their names until a little later, he did not want to be dishonest. He loved his wife and he had made a silent pact with himself never to do anything that would give her cause to doubt his integrity.

They moved into the empty house that same night and slept on an air mattress that they had bought at Wal-Mart.

They cleaned the townhouse together, getting it ready for the delivery of their furniture and Michelle seemed much more relaxed and happy now that she was home. He could no longer spot the raw fear in her eyes that he had noticed on the drive north. He relaxed and he knew that it hadn't been a mistake to marry her.

For the first time in many years he was truly happy, a lucky man with a beautiful and loving wife by his side. "Too bad" he thought. "If they only had met years ago, how much different would his life have been?"

Their furniture was finally delivered and Eric had asked Michelle to check everything off from their master list. "If you could do this, I will tell the men where to generally put things," he had said to her.

Her disposition seemed to change almost like a flash flood and he was keenly aware of a deep anger that seemed to have welled up in her. From what, he could not imagine.

She was downright nasty, not only to him but also to the movers and at one point one of them asked Eric, "Hey buddy, how long have you been married?" When Eric responded that they had just been married, the man grinned broadly at him and said, "It looks like you have your work cut out for you then."

Michelle did not like how any of the furniture was placed and she insisted that many of the pieces be moved again according to her instructions. Most of the movers complied good-naturedly and Eric tipped them well for their help, much of which was well above and beyond the call of duty. After they had left, she still was not happy with the way things looked, but they were both exhausted from their long day and they decided to call it a night and go to bed. He noticed however, that she moved as far to her side of the bed as was possible and he in turn was careful not to touch her.

Eric gently spoke to Michelle the next day and said, "You know honey, you are probably going to want to make changes many times over, before we are both comfortable with the placement of everything. I would ask you to please not spend too much time on this now. We have many things to do before we need to leave to go back to Florida again in less than a week. So let's just live with things for a while and over time I am sure it will all get placed just exactly where you would like it."

She just looked at him then and said calmly, "Eric, I have asked you not to call me 'honey.' Why can't you remember this? I just hope your memory isn't slipping. I don't want to get stuck with a husband who, not only is so much older than I am, but who also can't seem to remember a simple request."

He felt really hurt by what she had just said but he decided not to make it an issue or respond to her.

They had to shop for the usual things all couples do when they move into a new home. One of the first items on their list was shower curtains as well as some other small things for the kitchen, but she had such difficulties in making decisions about simple choices, that he told her, "This is getting very frustrating for me Michelle, I think you need to go out and get these things on your own. This is taking far too long and we don't have the luxury of all that much time. Perhaps, we should do our shopping for these items separately. If we divide up the list, I believe that this would be a far more efficient use of our time."

She responded by saying that she thought what he had just told her was nasty and disrespectful and she flatly refused to go out on her own.

Eric couldn't for the life of him figure out what had been so disrespectful about what he had suggested and when he asked her about it, she just shrugged and said it wasn't so much what he had said, but the tone of voice that bothered her. He thought about that and decided that perhaps he had been a little harsh.

Eric thought it best that he should now go and buy these items himself, since she flatly refused to go, but when he brought them home and proudly showed her his purchases, she did not like a single one of them, and in order to keep the peace he returned most, but she still complained bitterly about the few things he decided to keep.

After their return to Florida, when all the legal paperwork for the sale of his house was completed, Eric thought that a small vacation would do them both a world of good.

They spent a few days at her parents' house, to swim and

relax in their pool and later, on the drive northbound they visited them at their cottage in Northern Florida for a couple of days.

They also decided to visit Michelle's brother on their way north. Mitch, a gay man, lived in Atlanta and was one of her family members Eric had not met. He had been unable to come to their wedding and he sounded like one of the more interesting members of her family, one that Eric had looked forward to meeting.

They enjoyed a pleasant lunch together while Mitch related some very witty and interesting stories about his work as an interior decorator.

There seems to be something wrong here though, Eric thought, while he closely observed the relationship between brother and sister. He had been surprised back in Clearwater when Michelle did not seem very close to her family, but he concluded that they probably spoke and saw each other more often than he had been aware of.

With Mitch, things were different. Since he lived out of state, Eric thought that she would have been more demonstrative and more affectionate with her brother. Earlier, she had told him of a somewhat strained relationship between them in the past.

Eric had made reservations to stay for a few days in Cabin #10, at the small mountains resort in North Georgia where their relationship had begun.

He had tried to keep this a surprise for her but when he finally told her about it, she seemed a lot less excited about spending a little time there together then he had thought.

During their short stay there, she had seemed strangely distracted and the rekindling of those feelings they had discovered for each other on their first visit there, never reoccurred.

Even when together, they re-read the stuff they had written in the guest book only six short months ago, their first time there. When he hoped that they would rediscover love together, her behavior did not put his mind at ease.

"Michelle," he had said to her when they were just a little south of Pittsburgh, "I feel a little sick, feverish and weird. It could be something I ate, or else a flu bug. It is getting late and I have been driving all day. I would like to get home before midnight if we could. I know I promised you that we would stop over in Erie to spend a little time with your friend Margaret, but could we please skip this?"

She began to object but he cut her short and called Margaret's number on his cell phone, hoping that she would not be home. She did not answer and he was relieved.

Michelle asked him to call her back and to leave a message, something he had not wanted to do. He objected and said, "Look Michelle, we are just an hour away from Erie, if she is not home now, she is not likely to be back in time for us to touch base with her."

He made the call only because he was tired of arguing with her and he didn't feel at all well. It seemed so much easier to let her have her way and he was just too exhausted and too sick to care.

They passed Erie on I-90 and he let out an inaudible sigh of relief. Margaret hadn't called back!

When they were about twenty miles east of Erie, his cell phone rang. Dammit, he thought, I should have turned the stupid thing off.

Of course it was Margaret and when he told her where they were, she begged him to turn around at the next exit.

He let out a long sigh. He did not want to disappoint his bride and asked her friend at what exit they should meet.

They met her at some hamburger joint and he ordered some food for them. After listening to their chit chat for two hours, he finally decided that he had enough of this and he said that they would have to leave now. "I am exhausted," he said, "and we still have about four hours of driving ahead of us." It was now getting close to midnight.

To his surprise, Michelle for once did not object. They said goodbye to Margaret who asked Michelle to come back soon for a longer visit.

Little did Eric realize then, how soon that would be.

They arrived home after three in the morning and Eric spent the rest of that week recuperating from the flu.

Chapter
SEVEN

It was a cool morning in early June. Eric had taken a long and hot shower and let the scalding water warm the frigidness that he felt in his body. He had not wanted to turn on the exhaust fan in the bathroom. It was a bit noisy and he preferred the quiet of this early morning.

The bathroom windows as well as those of the master bedroom, overlooked a dense forest of birch trees and the changing spring colors of the foliage was spectacular. At first, he had started to see small buds appearing only a week or so ago, but now, those buds had turned into tiny leaves and everything all of a sudden had become a dense burst of green. The whitish grey barks of the birches were more starkly defined against the clear blue morning sky. "Oh, how beautiful nature could paint," he thought.

The bathroom mirrors had begun to steam up quite badly. The lady who had represented the builder during their walk-thru had warned them about always making sure that the exhaust fan was on. Oh well, Eric thought, a little damp vapor once in a while isn't going to hurt the paint too much and that may well be the price we sometimes have to pay for a little quiet contemplation.

This was actually the first morning that he felt a little more like himself. "God," he thought, "that flu bug really got to me." But now finally, he felt rejuvenated and more whole again. Isn't it interesting how your feelings change after a fever breaks? he thought. There was definitely a different energy, like the body knows it has healed itself and is now rejoicing in its wholeness.

He turned the steaming water off and grabbed around the shower curtain to find his bath towels. He had installed two white enamel hooks, just so he could reach around the corner quickly and grab his towels without dripping all over the tile floor. He would only have to open the shower curtain a little bit and keep the shower stall hot and steamy as long as possible.

To his surprise the towels were not there. He had been so sure he had put them there just before starting his shower. Was this one more of his senior moments? But when he stepped out of the shower stall, the towels weren't anywhere in the bathroom either.

"Michelle," Eric called to her, "where did my towels go?"

"Eric, I am doing the laundry and I decided to wash them as well," she called back.

"I understand that," he shouted now. "But couldn't you have replaced them?" She called back and remarked that she did not like the way he had said this.

"When you do not talk to me respectfully Eric, I will not respond to you!"

Eric became frustrated. Didn't she understand that calling to her from the bathroom, all dripping wet as he was, meant that he had to raise his voice a few decibels. He couldn't figure her out. Why was she so incapable of being more sensitive to what would ordinarily have been a simply courtesy? He most certainly would have been more considerate and replaced her towels. He ran out of the bathroom dripping wet and shivering, collected fresh towels from the linen closet, leaving a trail of wet footprints and ran back to the still warm and steaming bathroom to finish dressing.

They had breakfast together. He might as well have had breakfast by himself, he thought. She was obviously very angry with him, for what, he didn't know.

Shit, he thought, why should he apologize to her. He had not said anything that would have been offensive to anyone. She should be able to admit that it was simply an oversight on her part and he would have been happy with that and let it go. He would have given her a loving hug for being big enough to own up to it.

Several days ago, they had another argument about her not being happy to be living in Toronto. He had explained to her then as patiently as he could, that she had seen the townhouse he planned to buy and she had decided that she wanted to move with him. He had not put any pressures on her. Why was she now telling him that she did not like living in a big city, when in fact they were living in a suburb well north of the city? This area was still considered to be very rural, with many farms, green areas and with a large forest preserve in the back of their townhouse.

She responded then, that she had always wanted to live in Hendersonville, North Carolina, where her friends Doreen and John lived.

In desperation, he had finally said, "Michelle, if you really think you are going to be happier living there, why don't you move there then? I am committed to remain here for the next several years until I know that Jamie has been able to adjust to her new life. I want her to have every opportunity to love herself and both of her parents when she grows up. I am here, because I do not want her to become another unhappy and disturbed teenager. God knows there are enough of those. I made a promise to myself that I would do everything I could to continue to be a good parent to her. The fact that Jane and I are divorced does not change anything as far as I am concerned."

"Why don't you see if you can patch things up between you and Jane then?" she had responded angrily and he had become terribly frustrated about her inability to see and understand what he had tried so desperately to communicate to her.

"Because that marriage ended a long time ago Michelle. You and I are married now, I love you and I would like to believe that we can be happy together if we, each of us, do our work and continue to hold each other in a loving space."

He had kissed her then and said, "Please Michelle, we have only been back here a few days. Don't be so impatient and give it a little time." But she just pushed him away and he had begun to feel hopeless.

She had repelled all of his efforts to reconcile their differences and kept on nudging him about how unhappy she was and how it had been a bad choice for her to move here.

Now again, she indicated that she was not happy living here with him and that his disrespectfulness only made her want to leave more. Eric was flabbergasted.

That evening, after supper, he had explained to her one more time that all he had ever wanted was her happiness as well as his own and if she really was not happy here with him, she should move to where she thought she could find more happiness.

She had seemed very angry and bitter then and said that

she would leave early the following morning and that she would stop in Erie first to discuss her problems with her friend Margaret.

"I will sleep in the guest bedroom tonight Eric. I do not think that we should continue to sleep in the same bed as long as you keep telling me to leave."

He had been totally unprepared for her strange behavior and he felt terribly hurt and violated for how she was changing and turning the things he had said to her. He now began to wonder if she was actually that kind of a nasty person or were there other problems? Could it have something to do with a hormonal imbalance? Was she going through menopause? In that case, he would have to learn to make allowances.

He did not sleep much that night. Too many questions and not enough answers. When he heard her readying herself to leave early the next morning, he went down the stairs and said, "Michelle if you leave now, don't ever think that I will take you back. I think we need to talk this through, but if you insist on leaving, I want your keys back as well as my credit card. You have your own card which you can use. I will no longer pay your bills, because as far as I am concerned, this marriage is over."

She threw him the keys and the card and angrily and defiantly slammed the door behind her.

Eric was convinced that she would be back after she had reflected about it some more and after she had time to cool off.

He was very wrong however. She had not phoned him and when he finally called Margaret in Erie a few days later to find out where she was and if she was alright, because he had been worried about her, she told him that Michelle had left there very early that morning to spend some time with her friends in Hendersonville.

Eric had met Doreen and John when he and Michelle had visited with them on their way back to Toronto. He decided to phone Doreen before Michelle would get there. He hoped to get a better understanding from her as to what, if anything was wrong with his wife and if something could be done.

Doreen told him then that she had known Michelle for quite some time and it was her opinion that Michelle would need to remain on medication in order to function in a way where close and loving relationships were possible. They talked for a little while longer and before Eric hung up, she made him promise to phone Michelle in a few days, giving her enough time to work through some of what was bothering her.

After he got off the phone with Doreen, Eric sat for a very long time in deep thoughts. He tried very hard to get in touch with his own feelings, something that had never been very easy for him. What was it that he was feeling now? His wife was ill, of that there was little doubt, but was that reason enough to break up this marriage, a marriage for which he had held such hope? He wondered if his love for her would enable him to deal with her idiosyncrasies. Could he at his age still really love her that much?

Chapter
EIGHT

When Eric phoned several days later, Michelle seemed to be happy to hear from him, but to Eric it appeared that she had totally accepted what had transpired between them almost too casually. He thought, "She is unwilling to accept even the slightest bit of responsibility for what has happened."

Perhaps it was too soon, Eric concluded. He decided that it was better not to talk about what had occurred between them and instead he talked for a bit about meaningless things.

What a totally useless phone call, he thought. They had just been filling in time and then, almost as if by prearranged code, they ran out of meaningless things to say to each other, they said goodbye and hung up. He had yet again missed out on an opportunity to deal with some of their issues that seemed to have been responsible for their rift. Should he just overlook what she had done? But his pride or his ego or both would not tolerate this.

That phone call, he thought, was so completely inadequate. He wished now that he hadn't called her at all. He wouldn't call again, he decided. That way, it would be so much easier to get used to not having her around.

He pushed the thoughts of her firmly from his mind. He did miss her terribly, but by not talking to her it would be easier to forget her.

"Get on with your life," he thought. "Keep busy. But with what?" He was retired now and the things he routinely did, didn't even take up half a day. What would he have done with the balance of the days, if she'd been there with him? This didn't make sense, he concluded, to remain in a relationship, just to fill up the balance of each day. Surely, he could find more useful and productive ways to live.

He briefly thought about visiting David and his family in California, but he did not want to burden them. He knew, once he was out there by himself, they would grill him about his plans and how he was going to resolve this latest fiasco with his new bride.

He would like to spend some more time with his grand-daughters, he thought. They were growing up so quickly and he hardly knew them. Maybe he should try to be closer to them, but this was difficult with them being so far away.

He resolved his dilemma by promising himself to try to stay in touch with them by phone more often, but it seemed to him that oftentimes, the girls were always so busy and David could never talk to him very long because he continually needed to interrupt the conversation when he had to reprimand the girls about something or other.

The days moved by very slowly and when she had been gone for almost three weeks, he finally was beginning to adjust to life without her. He started to think differently then. He realized that most things in his life happened for the purpose of teaching him something. To make him grow as a person and he concluded that by necessity there had to be some suffering involved in this process. Through the ages, men had to endure pain for evolution to be possible, he decided. So be it, he thought, he would come out the better person for it. For the most fleeting of moments he had one of those rare insights, that perhaps his thinking could be tainted by his own perceptions, but then he quickly pushed this thought away from his mind.

It became easier now for him to fall asleep, when he finally retired for the night. He had not been sleeping well, but lately, he would sleep for six or seven hours uninterrupted and he felt well rested when he awoke.

Then one night she called him. He had been sound asleep. It was somewhere around midnight he guessed, when the phone rang.

"We need to talk," she said. She had been watching a musical program on TV. The music had been beautiful and inspiring. "Some of those haunting melodies," she said, "reminded me of you and the music you play on your keyboard.

"Eric, I do love you and I miss you. It is so hard to talk on the phone about our issues. The countryside out here is beautiful. I did buy some camping gear when I was in Erie. Why don't you come up here and we can go camping for a while? I am sure we will be able to better address some of our issues when we are closer to nature."

At first Eric didn't know what to say. Part of him wanted to reach out and take her in his arms. As if that would make everything all better. Then, he became more awake and started to think with some clarity. He was keenly aware that if he would say what he wanted and needed to say, that this would be coming from his ego self, his hurt self. It wouldn't be about holding her in a loving space, and it would have been accusatory and bitter, expressing all the disappointments and hurts he had felt over the past weeks.

He thought it strange that he was able to look at what was coming up. Almost like his other self, his inner self, was watching over him and making sure that he got it right. But oddly enough, what he told her did not at all express his feelings.

"Why should I travel all that way out there just to go camping with you? I have never camped before and I am not at all sure that I would like it. You were the one who left me Michelle. If you want to talk, you can certainly find your way back here. Drive back and we can talk." But he knew that he didn't mean it quite the way it came out.

They argued about that for a while back and forth and then she came up with another idea.

"Eric, why don't we meet in Erie? There is a beautiful camp site there, right on Lake Erie. That way I will be meeting you more than halfway."

He thought about that for a while and frankly, he was surprised that she had been able to come up with this conciliatory idea. That had not been her style. In the past, when she couldn't get her way, she would turn abusively aggressive and would blame him. Perhaps she has changed a little, he thought.

He complimented her for having thought about this and for suggesting it and they made plans to meet in Erie that following Friday at about four P.M.

After she had given him directions and the name of the campsite, they hung up.

Eric tossed and turned for most of that night. He couldn't decide if it had been wise to agree to meet her. Perhaps it would have been better to leave well enough alone, he thought. After all, he had now slowly become accustomed to dealing with life without her and he was just starting to be more comfortable with this newfound feeling. If things did not go well, he would have to start all over again.

He arrived about an hour too early, reserved a campsite, walked around a bit and waited impatiently in front of the camp office for her to arrive.

She was wearing a colorful little dress. It was one of his favorites. A small pretty floral print just short enough to expose her shapely legs, as she got out of her car. He wondered why she always wore those long ankle-length dresses and hid those pretty legs of hers.

She looked fresh and vulnerable to him and his resoluteness melted like wet snow on sunny warm pavement.

They drove their cars to the campsite and he helped her set up camp. She seemed to enjoy instructing him on what and how to do it and he let her help him, although she herself seemed to have difficulties following the directions which had come with the tent. They eventually got the tent up and he inflated the mattress he had brought.

By then it was almost seven and he decided it would be too late to start making a campfire to cook their meal.

"We could always leave that adventure until tomorrow," he said. "I saw a small little restaurant next to the campgrounds, suppose we walk there and buy some dinner."

It was Friday evening, the beginning of another summer weekend. The little restaurant was crowded with a lot of other campers, who so obviously had the same idea.

Their food finally arrived after a long wait, but it was surprisingly good. Eric had a glass of wine and she talked mostly about her experiences in North Carolina and of how beautiful the place was and oh, how she wished she could live there.

Nothing was said about her sudden departure from Toronto or her behavior which had led up to it.

Eric did not want to spoil their first meal together in many weeks, so he listened to her and patiently waited for an opportunity to raise those issues, but it never came to that. She did not seem to want to go there.

"Oh well," he thought, "there will be lots of time for that later."

They bought ice cream cones from the stand next to the restaurant and walked back to the campsite, quickly licking their cones before the warm summer night would melt the ice cream. Campfires were already evident everywhere now and the camp had become very crowded. All of a sudden it seemed that tents had sprouted up on every available little plot and where there had been a lot of empty spaces before between their campsite and the next, now it seemed that their tent and their neighbor's were almost touching.

If he had any thoughts of intimacy or, if he had planned to talk about their issues privately, he quickly had to abandon these ideas and again he hoped that there would be a better opportunity in the next day or so.

Eric made his first campfire ever that night, but he had expert help from his next door neighbor, who guided him every step of the way after he had wasted almost all of their kindling wood and matches on several unsuccessful attempts.

It was a beautiful and warm summer's night. There were countless stars visible overhead and even with the light of the many fires around them, Michelle was able to name and point out many of the star formations. Eric admitted that he knew very little about astrology, and she seemed happy with the opportunity to instruct him.

They sat by their campfire and they talked about many

different topics, always being careful to avoid the things that he, with his customary impatience, had wanted to talk about straight away, but that she, apparently wanted to steer clear of.

They were now both getting very tired after the long drive, and the strain of avoiding to talk about the very reason for them being together became evident. They felt awkward of going to sleep together in the same tent, so they unwittingly kept putting off the inevitable.

He couldn't explain why he felt that way, but he thought that it had something to do with the fact that he had worked so very hard for the past three weeks in thinking of life without her, in trying to forget her, that to include her now seemed a strain.

Finally, when most of flames of the campfires had diminished to soft glowing ashes, when the laughter of the many campers had become sporadic and the barking of dogs was no longer distinguishable, they moved inside their tent. He kissed her gently on her forehead. She responded more passionately than he had expected, but Eric was too confused and too preoccupied. All he wanted to do was to kiss her goodnight.

He hadn't wanted to make her feel rejected, but he also did not want to encourage her. He didn't know how to tell her that, how to explain to her what he felt. He was afraid it would come out all wrong, that she would not be able to understand it, so he said nothing and went to sleep, leaving her to her own thoughts.

He could hear loud snoring coming from the neighboring tent and it bothered him to sleep in such close proximity to others. He fell asleep thinking that this was yet another reason why he disliked camping.

He awakened to the unfamiliar and pungent smell of

burning wood. There must be some campfires already burning, he thought. He presumed people were cooking their breakfast. The smell gave him an appetite and he decided to see if he could get his own campfire going.

He quietly lay there, looking at her for a long time. She had such a beautiful face, he concluded. He couldn't figure out why her personality had become such a stark contradiction to that sweet face. She looked so peaceful laying there, her hair all touseled with sleep.

Then she began to stir, opening her eyes slowly and looking around, almost as though she was trying to remember where she was. He caught her eyes and she smiled at him. That smile of hers, which had the potential of lighting up an entire room, that smile, which could squelch the furor of a fighting battalion in one instant.

"Good morning Eric, how did you sleep?"

He smiled back at her. "Well enough," he responded. "At times though, I didn't know if you were the one snoring or if it was our next door neighbor," he wisecracked.

Sometimes she did snore a little and because he was a light sleeper, it would wake him. Then he would speak to her gently and ask her to roll over on her side and she would obediently turn without waking up.

He did eventually get their campfire going. Eric, not having any camping experience at all, had brought a small metal grill with him, which he thought he could simply place on top of the wood logs to cook their meals on. He had taken eggs and sausages from the cooler and he used an extra log to keep the small frying pan more level. Everything went well until one log began to burn more fiercely than the others and his small level plateau collapsed. Then the small metal grill began to tip over and before he was able to level things off, their breakfast wound up in the ashes.

With his ego now somewhat deflated, Eric grinned and admitted to Michelle that he was neither a seasoned camper nor a rocket scientist.

"What makes you think a rocket scientist would do any better with the equipment you brought?" she asked smiling. They both laughed. The kind of healthy laughter that comes from somewhere deep within and is completely different from the laughter evident when one is poking fun at someone. That good-natured laughter seemed to finally break the ice between them.

They scraped the ashes from their breakfast, although Eric swore that it was the other way around and that they scraped their breakfast from the ashes. They declared to each other that these had been the best sausages they had ever tasted.

Eric decided that if they ever went camping again, he had better invest in some proper equipment. He would go to a specialty place, he thought, not to Wal-Mart, but a place where he could get proper advice in learning all about life in the outdoors.

After they had cleared away their breakfast things, Michelle suggested that they visit the park which ran along the shores of Lake Erie.

"It is such a beautiful day Eric. We can drive into the park, park the car somewhere and go for a nice long walk along the shoreline. We might even find a secluded spot where we can sit and discuss our issues."

They discovered a lovely spot, on a little stretch of sandy dunes, overlooking the lake. After they were seated on the warm sand, Eric wanted to charge right into the things he had wanted so much to talk about ever since their arrival, but Michelle said, "Please Eric, let's just sit for a while and enjoy this. It is so nice and peaceful. See how the sun is making a shimmering path on the water and when these small clouds overhead float by, their shadows seem to create a patchwork design on the lake. How wonderful nature is to provide us with this view."

"Michelle, I am not really in the mood to look at and admire nature right now. I cannot enjoy this as long as I am focused on the problems we have been having. My mind cannot switch on and off like that. These issues I believe cannot be resolved just by appreciating nature," he said somewhat smugly.

He could almost sense the change in her. He had obviously said or done something that had annoyed her, but he couldn't for the life of him figure out what it was. Her eyes had lost some of their softness which had been there earlier.

It hadn't of course occurred to him that he could have waited a while longer. After all, he had already waited so long, what would a few more minutes have mattered now?

"Michelle," he forged ahead not caring, "why did you leave?"

"Because I love nature and I do not like big cities."

"But you knew that Toronto was not some little town. I took you there several times before you decided to marry me and I even had you pick out the color scheme for the townhouse. Besides, we actually live in the country. There are lots of farms not more than a half mile north of us and the back of our place overlooks a forest. I do not exactly call this big city living. Besides, when you made your decision to move with me, you knew that the key reason for me moving from Florida was to be closer to Jamie. You asked me then if this was to be permanent, and I told you truthfully that it would have to be for at least a couple of years."

"Another reason why I was unhappy and left was because you broke your promises to me Eric," she responded now, angrily.

He was keenly aware that her response did not deal in any way with what he had just said.

"How have I not kept my promises to you?" he demanded more harshly than he intended.

"You promised that we would continue with the Imago program," she answered.

He had watched some tapes a while back and they had become interested in what it had to offer to improve communications between couples. They had taken a weekend seminar together but he had not been very impressed by it. He had found their methods too clinical, almost mechanical and somewhat dehumanizing. He had told her so, but he was not at all sure if indeed he had said that he was interested in taking more courses.

They argued about her calling it a promise as he patiently explained that there simply had been no such promise. He wanted to know why she would purposely distort that reality.

Although by now he realized that she had some emotional problems, he was not yet ready to accept this reality, and to make allowances by learning to stretch.

They were getting nowhere this way, he realized. This wasn't even what he had wanted to talk to her about. He had wanted her to know that based on what Doreen had told him over the telephone, their life together and their happiness as a couple could only become a reality if she sought medical help and would remain on some sort of medication to correct the chemical imbalance in her system.

"Doreen told me she never said that," Michelle responded in anger.

Then, he finally told her, "I will not take you back into my life unless you get medical help Michelle. That's it. This is my bottom line."

At last, she grudgingly agreed to see a doctor. "Not a psychiatrist," she said. "I will not be medicated to please any man."

Eric realized that this was the best he could hope for at this moment. He thought that once she had been referred to a psychiatrist who might prescribe medication, she would be obliged to take it. He was convinced that this was the only thing which could save their marriage. She was wonderful to be with when she was fine, but when she got into that other self, living with her became totally unbearable.

They finally agreed to drive back to Toronto the following morning and he promised himself to be patient and compassionate with her.

Chapter
NINE

If, after this, Eric had high hopes about Michelle settling down to be a happy loving partner and soulmate living in Toronto, he was sadly mistaken. He couldn't quite understand why she seemed so terribly unhappy. They lived in a nice place, she didn't have to work any longer and they had the luxury of being able to travel whenever and wherever they wanted. Why had she agreed to marry him?

He made an appointment with his family doctor who, after seeing her, referred her to a specialist. Unfortunately there was a long waiting period before she could get in to see him and Eric thought it might be good for her state of mind if they could spend some time camping and traveling.

"Michelle," he told her one morning during breakfast, "you mentioned some time ago that your descendants had moved from New Brunswick to Louisiana. How would you like to visit the Canadian Maritimes? Perhaps we can make a little adventure about discovering your ancestry. We can spend several weeks doing some camping and traveling there. Your appointment with the specialist is not for another four weeks and that would give us lots of time. The summer is a great time to visit Eastern Canada."

"That would be wonderful Eric. It would give me a chance to get in touch with my Acadian roots. I haven't seen much of Canada yet and this will give me a better understanding of the country I intend to call my home." There it was again, this wonderful smile of hers which could disarm the hangman.

Eric was more than a little pleased. Was she at long last becoming more realistic? Were things finally beginning to sink in with her that it didn't matter so much where they lived. . . . He could be happy almost anywhere, he thought, as long as their relationship was solid.

They made plans together to leave as soon as possible. He became a little disappointed that she did not seem to want to become more involved in the places they were planning to visit, when he pointed these out on the many maps he had obtained from the Motor League.

"Maps and I don't get along too well. I really find it difficult to understand them. I am a visual person Eric and I can relate better when we drive through these areas," she had said.

He accepted this and thought: Life would be very difficult for her if, as her friend Doreen had told him, she had perceptual problems. He tried to put himself in her place and could now better understand how and why she would become so terribly defensive at times. Fear of not being able to perceptually understand things must be a terrible thing, he concluded and he promised himself he would be more compassionate and understanding.

He remembered now, when years ago, he had worked with kids in the school system as a volunteer. He had learned then to have more empathy with their difficulties and he knew if they felt even a trifle inferior, it would take a long time to win their confidence back.

While they were traveling, on the surface of things, their relationship seemed fine. She was happy most of the time and although he often had difficulties in detecting genuine love and warmth toward him, it was good to see her take a more active part in their lives. They shared a number of experiences together and enjoyed talking about these little adventures to other couples they met at the various different campsites.

He learned quickly though, that he could not depend on her to help him navigate with driving directions. On the few occasions when he did ask her for help, they invariably wound up in the wrong area. Most of the time, he would remember her problems and would let it go, but sometimes, when he forgot, they would argue about it and she could become very nasty and ugly.

Eric assumed that this was her way of feeling safer with him. When she was able to vigorously defend her perceived shortcoming, mostly by abusing him verbally. He simply gave up asking her to help him navigate. It just seemed so much easier to write out his directions before they left in the morning. He would then know precisely where and when to turn.

They returned home after three weeks of traveling and camping and Michelle seemed genuinely happy to be back in their comfortable townhouse.

Three days after their return, during breakfast, she looked at him and he was shocked to see anger and hatred in her eyes again. Or was it fear?

"Eric, I told you before that I hate living in this big city.

It is not were I feel I belong. Why can't we sell this house and move to North Carolina?"

He was shocked. This had come out of nowhere.

"Honey, when we moved here a few months ago, you knew that this would be where we would be living for a couple of years. At least until Jamie will be better adjusted. As a teenager, this is a difficult time for her. After she has been in high school a few years we can revisit this moving idea of yours. We just came back from our little vacation. Please be patient for a while longer. If after you have given it a good try and you still want to move, I will help all I can. I myself am committed to remain here for a while, but if you are really not happy here, then in the long run, this would make me very unhappy as well and as long as we both cannot be happy as a couple, it would be better for you to move to your own place."

"I told you many times," she almost screamed it at him. "Don't call me HONEY! You call all your waitresses Honey. I am not your waitress."

"Come on Michelle," he said, "this is really silly. I made a simple mistake."

"I know what you are doing," she countered. "You figure, 'as long as I can keep her here for a while, she will become used to living here.' You are trying to keep me imprisoned. I had been forewarned about you. You are a fucking control freak."

For a moment he thought she had gone off the deep end. He had never been talked to this way by anyone.

He struggled to keep control over his emotions. Finally he said, "Michelle if you really feel that you have to live in North Carolina, if you love it there so much, then you must go. I suggest you go out there, rent a little place and find yourself a job. See how you like it. If after you have tried it for a while and you haven't changed your mind about living there, I will ship your belongings and your furniture to you. You have enough money from the sale of your house in Florida and after a while, you could buy a place of your own. It makes absolutely no sense for us to remain together if you are this unhappy. If after a few months you should change your mind, and would want to come back here, we could leave that door open."

"How do I know that I can trust you to ship my things to me?" she said.

"You could always come back to make sure you get all that belongs to you," he answered fiercely. He was now desperately fighting to keep control over his anger. He almost thought that this was another one of his nightmares and that he would soon wake up and everything would be the way he had so often envisioned his life should be.

She parlayed back a few more nasty remarks, but Eric decided not to remain in the same room any longer. It was best, he thought, to remove himself. He went out to the garage to wash his car.

When he returned, he thought it best to tell her, that if she did decided to leave, she would have to deed the house back in his name.

"Michelle, you do know that based on our prenuptial agreement the house was deeded as joint ownership, even though I paid for the entire amount. Of course the agreement was not based on just being married for a few months. So if you are serious about leaving, then I will speak to the lawyer and see what is required in order to change the deed."

"I will not sign over anything to you Eric, until I too

have first seen a lawyer. I do want to find out what my rights are."

His heart turned to stone. Had she planned this from the very beginning? How could he have made such a horrible mistake? Was she just another little gold-digger? Perhaps she had not really been in love with him at all? Or maybe she had not been sure of this? There had been so little time before they decided to get married. That was of course entirely possible. She had probably thought that if she discovered that she really didn't love him and if things didn't work out well between them, she could always leave and then realize a handsome benefit by demanding that he pay her for half of her interest of the townhouse.

Eric shook his head. As if that action, all by itself, would chase away all of those hideous thoughts.

He had always hated dealing with lawyers. During his whole life and even in the business world, he had never met one that was genuinely interested in creating a win-win situations.

That afternoon, he decided to phone his lawyer to find out how much this could eventually cost him. He was told that because of the prenuptial agreement, she could possibly be entitled to half his house.

Initially he was devastated. Why had he been so gullible? He hadn't known her all that long before they were married. Why had he been so accommodating to give her half of his house? He should have put some kind of timeframe into the prenuptial. Should have, would have or could haves don't count now, he decided. There was no point in these kinds of mind games. Perhaps, she would settle for less. He hadn't even spoken to her about how much exactly she expected from him. Possibly, this had not been really what she wanted. Because of her inability to clearly define issues, was he drawing the wrong conclusions? They needed to talk frankly about this, before he started to get all this crazy stuff into his head, but how do you talk to someone frankly and honestly when they have difficulties with conceptualizing things?

Later that afternoon Michelle's father phoned Eric on his cell phone. He wanted to know what was going on. Eric hadn't expected the call. He didn't think that Michelle had talked to him about their difficulties. He didn't see any point in telling him about what Michelle wanted to do. The old man would side with his daughter of course. Eric was sure that he himself would naturally support his own daughter's position, so he didn't say much and just listened.

"Eric," her father had finally said, "please make sure that she goes and gets counseling."

Michelle had obviously spoken to him about their previous difficulties.

Eric felt like saying to him, "I think she needs more than counseling," but he resisted that temptation and after he had promised that he would try to talk to her, they hung up.

Why hadn't anyone in her family ever discussed with him that there was a problem and more importantly what that problem was? He probably would still have married her, but he would have known better what to do and how to help her.

Michelle made dinner that night and Eric asked her if she wanted to join him in a glass of wine.

"No Eric, I do not and I don't want you to have one either."

"Why not?" he demanded more forcefully than he had intended. "Why would you object to me having a glass of wine with dinner?"

"Because my ex-husband always drank more than he should and it always led to troubles between us."

"Michelle, that just doesn't make sense. One small glass of wine is hardly going to make me act irresponsible, besides, I wish you would stop comparing me to anyone else. Whatever happened was then, it has nothing to do with me. Please don't bring the past into our relationship."

He poured himself a glass. It occurred to him later that under normal circumstances he would probably not have poured a full glass, but he had this feeling. His ego was screaming at him: "Screw her!"

They sat down to dinner and he told her about her dad's call.

"I do not need to go and see another counselor. I have gone to too many of them already and all they do is tell you that something different is wrong with you. They all tell you something else and they just confuse the hell out of me. They label you and so many of them are so screwed up themselves, that I just don't have confidence in them any longer. Besides, they charge a lot and I do not have insurance coverage. By the way, Eric, that's another thing you promised to look after, which you haven't done."

"Honey, I told you that I looked after that the day we came back from our trip. You probably forgot. You do have medical coverage now," he said. "But you are probably right, they do not as a rule pay for that kind of counseling."

"Again with the honey," she said. "How come you can't remember it when I ask you a simple request? Maybe the age difference is the reason why we don't get along better. My girlfriend warned me not to marry a man who was so much older."

"Michelle," he said, trying to ignore her snide remarks,

"why don't you phone the specialist to see if you can see him sooner?"

"Stop always telling me what to do Eric, I am not a child."

"Why don't you phone your dad back then," he said. "You can explain to him yourself why you do not want to go and get the help you need and why you want to move to North Carolina."

Later that evening, he realized that it had been a mistake to suggest this. She did make the call to her father and after the conversation was over, she slammed down the phone and went completely out of control. It was as though he had picked up a stray cat somewhere and whenever he tried to stroke it, she would purr, but when he stopped, he would be bitten and clawed the very moment he put her down. Putting her down, all of a sudden took on a different meaning for him, he realized and he had to be very careful how and what he said to her when she was in one of her mood swings.

Eric finally understood, that it was quite futile to argue with her any longer. After the dishes where put away he suggested that she take a nice warm bath. He said, "Having a hot bath always makes you feel better Michelle, and if you like, I will bring you up some hot tea. You will be more relaxed and we can talk later."

He finally had intended to ask her straight out what it was she was after and how much it would take to get her to move to North Carolina. This was no way to live, he concluded.

When she came down later, she indeed seemed more relaxed. They sat down. He on the small love seat, but instead of joining him as he had hoped, she immediately sat down on the opposite chair. She apparently did not want to be too close. She must have intuitively guessed what was coming and wanted to keep a safe territorial space between the two of them.

Eric thought about this and decided that it was probably better that way. At least he could see her face and watch for any adverse reactions. He realized, that what he was about to say, had to be put very delicately.

"Michelle," he began, "This way of living together cannot continue much longer. I want to spend the rest of my remaining years living in peace and harmony. What is it that you really want?"

"I want half the house," she said. "The prenuptial gives me that entitlement."

Eric could feel the shift coming over him.

All of a sudden, out of nowhere, he recalled a vision of his mother pleading with his dad, when the Gestapo had ordered them out of their house in Holland. "Please Jakob, let me at least take some of my silverware?" Tears were streaming down her face but all his dad could say was that she could not take anything. "It simply isn't safe," he had said.

Eric could feel the blood rushing to his face. He stood up from the love seat and came over to where Michelle was sitting. He took her wrists in both of his hands and more forcefully than he had intended, he pulled her up out of her seat. Then, he hissed in a voice that seemed not to belong to him, toneless and totally devoid of any emotions, "You are nothing but a cheap little cunt. I cannot consider you my partner any longer, knowing that you are trying to rip me off. I feel betrayed and I do not want to live with you as your husband under the same roof a minute longer. I want you to go upstairs, pack a bag and leave this house immediately. I will pay for a hotel until we can get your things moved to North Carolina. In the meantime, you can see a lawyer who can tell you about your fucking precious rights."

"You are hurting me Eric. Are you trying to break my wrists?" she said. Raw, naked fear was now clearly visible in her eyes

He saw her fear and said, "I should hurt you a lot more, you deserve it, you bitch." For the briefest of moments he was tempted to take his hands around her neck and choke her and really hurt her, but he knew that he was not that kind of person. I won't stoop to that level, he thought to himself. No one can ever make me do this, no matter what they do to me. She does not have that kind of power over me. Certainly, she is not worth it.

He released her. She screamed for help hysterically then she ran up the stairs to his office phone and called 911. Her screaming sounded so terribly phony to him, so put on.

He heard her talk to the cops and alarm bells went off in his head. He picked up the downstairs phone extension to explain to them that his wife was not well, not quite acting herself, that she needed to take some medication to calm herself down, but of course they would not hear any of this. He was ordered to stay downstairs in a different room until they arrived.

When they came, they spoke to Michelle for a short time and he overheard her saying that he had been drinking.

They did not seem in the least interested to hear his explanations of what really did happen. He was handcuffed and pushed into a police cruiser like a common criminal.

When he complained that the cuffs were hurting him, he was told that the station, where he would be booked was not far and once inside, they would remove the cuffs.

Inside the station, when the cuffs were removed, he looked at his wrists and he noticed ugly red welts where the cuffs had been. Minutes later, he was read his rights, booked and escorted to a holding cell.

This was the first time in his whole life that he had seen the inside of a jail cell. He looked around sadly and pondered why God and men had found it so necessary to punish him. He had done nothing wrong.

It was then still too soon for Eric to fully understand, that all things happen for a reason; that everything that happens in this universe is for us to learn and to grow from. For this is how humanity will eventually evolve and how we inevitably will learn to love unconditionally and irregardless. How we will learn, that angry responses are mindless responses and are the causes of so much unhappiness in our world.

Chapter
TEN

He woke and sat bolt upright. For a brief moment he had no idea where he was. He didn't know what time it was or how long he had been asleep. By the way he felt, it couldn't have been much more than an hour at most. Had he just been having one of his bad dreams?

Then he became more fully awake, remembering and he knew he had not been dreaming. The little cot he was sitting on had a lumpy little mattress on it and it smelled like old clothing which hadn't been washed for many months. There was a small light in the corner of his little cell where the toilet was located.

He had to pee. It had become his habit to sit on the toilet when he peed. One of his former lady friends, a nurse, had suggested that he should sit down and instead of shaking his penis to eliminate the drops, he now wiped himself with toilet paper. She had said that it was more hygienic that way, but here, on this dirty toilet, he was not going to sit down. No fucking way.

"Isn't it interesting," he thought, "I have only been in jail for a couple of hours, not years, and it is already changing my personality. I am not yet an angry person, but I can easily see how jail can become a dehumanizing experience."

He didn't know what time it was. The little room was windowless and they had taken his watch and all of his personal belongings away from him, when they had booked him. He estimated it was about four in the morning. He couldn't have been asleep for very long, he guessed. He remembered being awake for most of the night. In the end, he had been so horribly tired, but his mind didn't want to give in, to allow him the opportunity to turn things off in his head and get some sleep. Thinking about her sleeping peacefully in his house, had made his blood boil over and over again.

They must have had some sort of a monitoring system in the cell. Eric had looked around, but he could not detect a camera, but shortly after he had urinated, someone had started talking to him through a speaker on the wall.

"Since you have not had time to get a lawyer," the voice said, "we have a lawyer who is on call here with the station. He is on the phone right now and if you would like to speak with him, just pick up the small handle hanging on the wall. He will be able to advise you of your rights and then you could be released early this morning. He does not cost you anything, because he works for the ministry. Go ahead and pick up the phone."

The man on the phone introduced himself and explained to Eric that if he preferred, he could remain in jail until he would be able to appear in front of a judge—he would then be released if he signed an undertaking that he would abstain from any communications with his wife and not to go near his house at any time, except in the company of a police officer to get some of his personal belongings.

"However, they could release you this morning, if you sign this undertaking at the station. They can only do this if you have had legal advice, which is why they asked me to speak to you." He went on to say that Eric would also have to sign a promise to appear on a specified date in court and, the lawyer said, "If you should break these undertakings, there would be very serious consequences."

Eric briefly thought about what the voice had told him and after he had carefully considered his options, he had to agree that the sooner he got out of there, the sooner he could get his own lawyers to get him vindicated.

By seven that morning they had returned his personal things to him and Eric requested that an officer meet him at his house by eight to get his car and some of his clothing and personal belongings.

He walked out of the police station into that early morning dew. A free man again. He thought about the many inmates who must have similar experiences and he now better understood just how imperfect the legal system was. How many of them had been innocent like him, accused of crimes far more serious than his? How many become outraged, angry and bitter toward the very society that had so mistreated them? Is it any surprise that some turn to crime, or worse, become terrorists to give a voice to their anger when no one seems to be listening?

He took a deep gulp of the fresh morning air and decided to walk the considerable distance to his house. It would take him no more than an hour at a fast pace, he figured and he was happy for the opportunity to be able to walk and have this exercise. Besides, he would not be able to meet the officer much before eight in any case.

When he met the police officer at his house, he was told to stay well back, while the cop rang the doorbell.

After some considerable time, Michelle answered the door in her housecoat. The officer explained what they had come for and she immediately complained about not having been forewarned. "This is very inconvenient for me," she said. "I was about to take a shower. I have an appointment later this morning. Can't he come back and give me some more notice?"

The officer responded that Eric was only allowed to take some of his personal belongings and that he probably wouldn't need much longer than ten minutes. "It can't take him much longer than that to get a few of his personal effects," he said.

As usual, Michelle had severe problems whenever she was not getting her way, but now she realized she was in the driver's seat and she was going to take maximum advantage of this opportunity.

She first asked to see a signed copy of the paper which stated that he was entitled to this one time visit. Then, she grudgingly stood aside to let them in.

While Eric went up the stairs to get some of his most urgently needed things, he overheard her talking to the officer.

"I do not have any money," she whined, "and if I cannot communicate with my husband any longer, how do I negotiate with him to get the cash for my half of the house?"

"You get a lawyer lady," the cop offered.

"I don't like lawyers and I don't see why I have to get one. Can I not talk to my husband directly while you are here?"

"No," he replied. "You don't seem to get it do you? He is not allowed to talk to you. Don't you understand! Your marriage is over now and you will need to get a lawyer who specializes in family law. The sooner you have an agreement in writing to settle things between the two of you, the sooner the courts will be able to step away from this and then you can both get on with your lives."

Eric didn't want to listen any longer to her bellyaching.

He rushed to pack some of his most essential things in a small bag and then he took the keys from his car. He was about to put his bag in the car, when the officer stopped him and said, "You can only take your personal effects. I cannot let you take your car unless your wife approves."

Eric came back inside from his garage, while the officer asked Michelle.

"No, he cannot take his car. His lawyer will need to contact mine. I want to get legal advice first."

Eric was asked to leave his house.

So that was that. He had no choice now but to call his brother-in-law from his cell phone and asked him for a ride to a car rental agency so he could make arrangements about renting a car. He waited by the curb with his small satchel in the early morning chill, feeling forlorn, bitter and angry.

She was playing hard ball, he decided and there was nothing he could do about it at this moment. His turn would come. In the meantime he needed to keep his nose clean and keep a cool head. To antagonize her or the cop wouldn't help him in the least.

He had a court date set in ten days to appear in front of a judge. He considered his options and thought, "I will get the best damn lawyer I can find. I am sure that this case will be thrown out of court. Once she understood from her own lawyer that she could be sued for false arrest, she would be a lot less arrogant to deal with." He would be very tough then in his negotiations with her.

He rented the car for ten days. He was convinced that he would have his car back by then, if not before.

He phoned the lawyer who had handled the house purchase for him and he explained what had happened.

"You will need a criminal lawyer, Eric, and also someone

who specializes in family law. I have a lawyer in this office, who works with me and he can handle the family law side for you. I also have a friend who practices criminal law. He is not a big gun, mind you, but I do not believe you need to pay five hundred dollars an hour to get a top-notch criminal lawyer. This is a very simply case and he will do a good job for you."

Eric phoned both lawyers and set up appointments to see them as soon as possible.

The next ten days went by excruciatingly slowly. He was able to stay at his sister's house instead of a hotel, but he couldn't find anything to keep himself busy with, except reading and he was very aware that he had serious problems in concentrating. He had not been allowed to take any of his office files nor his computer, so he could not do the usual things which would have kept his mind occupied at least for a portion of the time.

It was near impossible to do anything without thinking about the unfairness of it all. Sometimes he would be feeling very angry with Michelle and at other times he felt sorry for her.

She was in a foreign country, where she did not know many people. To be all by herself in the house, with her own thoughts and her memories, perhaps beginning to feel a little remorseful for what she had done. He wondered how she was holding up. From the early stages of their relationship he remembered that she could suffer from deep depressions.

The evening before the court hearing he received a call from the criminal lawyer. "Sorry Eric, I cannot be there myself tomorrow, but there really isn't too much I can do or say in any case. They will just ask you if you are guilty or not and then they will set a trial date. I have asked a friend of mine to appear on your behalf."

Eric was furious. "Don't you think this is a little late to let me know this?"

"I have to be at a different courthouse tomorrow. This case was on the books well before I took you on as a client. Don't worry Eric, I know what I am doing. It will be fine. They will only set the trial date tomorrow. Trust me on this one, I am your lawyer and it will all work out."

Eric thought, "I don't know if I can ever trust anyone again," and he went to his court date with some serious misgivings.

And it wasn't fine. The prosecutor who was to handle his case was away ill, and unfortunately for Eric, he had the file with him and they could not set a trial date without having his file. Since the court only sat each Monday, his case was remanded till the following week.

After spending considerable time at the courthouse trying to get further information, Eric left disgusted with the system and with his lawyer.

"Another week," he thought. "It is not the end of the world. It will be hard waiting this out, but next Monday, I will be vindicated."

He drove back to the car rental agency, to extend his rental agreement for another week.

He spoke to his lawyer a few days before his court appearance. "Eric," he said, "I made sure that this time they got the file back from that prosecutor who was ill and that your file was turned over to another prosecutor. I know her personally, and I am going to be there to make sure that this time we set a trial date for sure."

But again, they were unable to get a trial date. The prosecutor, who had received his file, had been too busy with another case which had gone much longer than expected. His case was once again remanded and turned over to yet another prosecutor.

That following Monday would be a holiday and the courts would be closed, so his case had to be remanded for two more weeks.

Eric now examined his lawyer's face more closely. He was a mousy, sad looking kind of a man with a shallow complexion. His skimpy hair of undeterminable color had a few droopy strands stuck to his forehead. He was wearing his legal regalia and it was almost comical to see him walk. He resembled a large black bird with his garments flapping around him like a pair of useless wings. So far as lawyers go, Eric thought, he had been about as useless as those imaginary wings of his.

It had now been six weeks since he had first been charged.

It was the middle of November and the temperature was getting progressively colder. Eric began to realize that he had not taken enough warm clothing to wear. He had been sadly mistaken when at first he had been overly-optimistic in his evaluations that this thing would be over in a few weeks. It seemed to be dragging on and on and Eric didn't know if this was due to the inefficiency of the court system or, was his lawyers dragging this out, so he could bill his clients for more and more time?

Michelle had finally hired a lawyer, but she had given him no instructions, even though apparently he had advised her to release Eric's car. Whenever Eric's lawyer phoned about getting his car back, he was told that her lawyer had severe difficulties in getting his client to take his advice.

Negotiations were going nowhere fast, and this could drag on indefinitely.

Eric had been living at his sister's house all this time and he was beginning to feel that he was overstaying his welcome. He sensed that it was time to go elsewhere and he decided to spend some time with his married daughter and her husband. He realized though that he should not remain there too long either. She had her own family concerns to deal with.

If only he could get his car back, and get some more of his clothing and his computer, he could drive to Florida and live on his boat until Michelle became tired of this cat and mouse game she was playing.

Finally, Eric told his lawyer, "I will accept no further delays. I will get myself another lawyer unless we get a trial date next Monday.

"Once we have a definite trial date, I want you to ask the judge to sign an order to release my car. Tell the judge that this situation is most unfair. If I had a trial date set and my car returned to me, I would at least have a place to stay without having to be a burden on anyone."

The next Monday, he finally got what he had wanted all along: A trial date for June the following year and an order to release his car.

Michelle inexplicably had shown up at the hearing and she requested that they be given permission to meet together in the presence of a professional counselor. It now seemed apparent that she preferred to see if their marriage could be saved through counseling and the judge approved her request.

When Eric went to pick up his car and when he collected his mail at the mailbox the very next day, he found a note from Michelle. It gave the name and phone number of a psychotherapist with her request that, based on the decision of the judge, he should make an appointment with this counselor as soon as possible.

Eric, more than a little confused, did so that very afternoon. He was able to get an appointment for Thursday, but when he arrived there, at the appointed time, Michelle was not there. He was told that she had departed for Chicago to spend the U.S. Thanksgiving holiday with friends there. Eric concluded that he had once again been wrong about her. It was apparent now, that she had only wanted *him* to get counseling, for what, he could not imagine. He assumed that she was now really convinced that he had assaulted her and that he consequently needed to deal with his anger by getting psychotherapy.

He decided not to waste any further time. The weather was getting quite cold now. Next week it would be December 1st already. Winter weather driving conditions could be expected at any moment. He would depart on Sunday for the drive to Florida and planned to winter over on his boat. He would at least have a place to live. The trial date was not till June and now, time was on his side. Michelle would get tired of the Canadian winters and she would want to get this thing settled. This time, he would let her chase him for a while.

Chapter
ELEVEN

He loaded his SUV up on Saturday afternoon. That previous day he had bought some plastic see-through filing cabinets. These were perfect, he decided. On the outside one could tell if they contained his tee shirts, sweaters or his trousers. The drawers could be pulled out on a track so he could more easily get to the items which might be located in the back of the drawers. By stacking his clothing, he would be able to pull out just what he needed, without having to unpack an entire suitcase or a duffel bag, which at times could be a problem on a small boat. The drawers fitted snugly in the back of his SUV without sliding. It was a neat arrangement and it would help to keep his things organized. His sailboat was only twenty-nine feet, with minimal storage places. This way, he could keep most of his things in his car and only take out what was needed when he needed it.

Michelle had finally also given permission to take his office files which fitted neatly next to his clothing.

Eric was very pleased with himself, when he looked at these arrangements and he was confident that he could live comfortably on board his boat this way for many months. He had bought a laptop to replace the bigger and clumsier computer and he had been able to transfer all of his files to his laptop.

It was the first of December, a very early Sunday morning when he quietly let himself out of his daughter's house. He hoped to complete the trip to St. Petersburg in two days, providing the weather would cooperate.

For the first time in many months he felt whole again. He was finally on his way to a place he could again call his own. A place, where he would have privacy, a place, where he didn't have to be concerned that he would offend anyone if he accidentally burped.

God it felt good to leave the city behind! He had been dreaming about living on board his boat for more than a month now, ever since he no longer had a place he could call his own.

There was hardly any traffic at that hour of the morning and he was making excellent time. He began to hum softly. It felt so good to take control of his life again, to finally feel free from all of the pain and frustration he had to endure. He already imaged himself scrubbing his decks while the warm Florida sun played on his back and chased away the winter chills.

The roads had been clear and dry, but just before he crossed the U.S. border it began to snow a little. It was mostly wet stuff, but the temperature had been dipping below the freezing mark and he was concerned that the roads might become slippery. He slowed down considerably and hoped that the weather would improve as he worked his way south.

He thought about Michelle. He wondered where she was. Had she remained in Chicago, or was she driving back to Toronto? Perhaps, she and her friend were driving south to spend Christmas in Florida.

He thought about her a lot. Life could have been so beautiful if they had been able to remain together. What had she hoped to benefit from all this? Surely she would have been better off in every way, if she had not done what she did. What on earth was wrong with her?

He went on like this for quite some time, until common sense told him that there was no point in pondering all this. He would never be able to find these answers and it only served to upset him. He certainly did not want to lose his newly-found freedom by again becoming a prisoner of his past. He began to realize that his mind was not being overly kind to him by keeping him thinking this way and he resolutely decided that he did not want to lose this feeling of wellness that he had felt ever since he got up early that morning.

By about ten he stopped for breakfast. The snow had turned to rain now and he was making a little better time again.

"Why worry about that?" he thought. His whole life, he realized, had been about accomplishing certain goals within certain time frames. It wouldn't matter if he had to drive a little longer that evening! Time, he decided was in itself timeless, just like answers were often hidden in the questions themselves and every process was processless.

"Just enjoy the ride and this wonderful feeling of freedom," he decided.

By the time he had crossed the Virginia border, he was bone weary and decided to call it a night. He had stopped earlier to eat a light meal at dinner and after he checked into the motel, he watched television for the briefest of moments and then crashed almost instantly.

He woke at four the following morning as he had done

for so many mornings. He laid there for a while and thought of her.

He had been so very angry with her for quite a long time now and many of his previous thoughts had been about getting even with her, teaching her a lesson, but now, he noticed a slight difference in his thoughts. He was no longer feeling sorry for himself or feeling the victim, and his anger for her was starting to subside. He now began to see his anger as his own affliction, and instead he was beginning to feel sorry for her. Compassionate was probably a better way to explain what he felt. He couldn't quite figure out why this was so, but he liked not feeling his anger. This felt so much better, he decided.

He jumped in the shower, had some of that horrible room coffee and was on the road by five.

It was a clear morning, and the roads were dry now. Every once in a while, as he dropped down into the valleys below, he would have to slow down because of a patches of early morning ground fog.

He had always enjoyed driving at this hour, he remembered. That little bit of time just before dawn. He loved discovering that little patch of light, as it appeared ever so small, ever so faint at first on the horizon and then it began to spread, almost as though someone had slowly raised the dimmer mechanism of a light switch.

The sun came up to his right, at first a red ball hanging at the far end of the horizon, and then, majestically rising over the Virginia mountains.

A rebirth in a sense, just like his own. A whole new day and in a way, a whole new beginning for him as well.

He had hoped to arrive at the marina, where his boat had been in dry dock, before they closed up for that evening.

Now he realized that by the time he would get to St. Petersburg, it would be too late to launch Final Draft and he decided to sleep over in Gainesville. It seemed so much more sensible to arrive at the marina bright and early the following morning.

The sun was just beginning to set as he parked his car at the Marriot. He got out and took a deep gulp of the warm and comforting air.

It felt good to be back in Florida!

He thought of her again then. Too bad, that she wasn't here to share these moments with him.

When would he stop thinking about her? When would he stop including her in his life? he wondered.

Chapter
TWELVE

He had reserved a slip for Final Draft at the Harborage Marina, without ever seeing the marina complex. He knew roughly where it was located from having passed by there once or twice, but he actually had never been there and he didn't know anything about their facilities. He had looked them up on the Net and it seemed to be pretty much what he wanted.

It was located on the inner harbor, right on Tampa Bay. There were a number of Coast Guard vessels stationed permanently in the outer harbor, and the view from the breakwater, which separated the outer from the inner harbor, was to say the least quite spectacular. The concrete breakwater also served the dual purpose of keeping the boats, which were tied up on slips behind it, from rocking a lot during rough weather. Located at the extreme end of this breakwater were two unisex toilets with showers.

From where Eric's boat was tied up, it was perhaps a few minutes walk, up and across the concrete breakwater to the toilets and showers and he always enjoyed the view on early mornings, whenever he looked out over the bay, as he went to take his shower. To actually call them showers was perhaps a slight overstatement. He compared it to a spring drizzle of almost, but not quite warm water, but it served its purpose.

To do his laundry however, meant walking quite a distance to the office complex area and the main buildings, which were located on the south side of Third Avenue. This was also the area where the public phones were located, but he decided to get his own telephone installed on board, which would give him access to the internet as well. Since he figured he was going to be living on board for quite a while, he wouldn't feel quite so cut off from the rest of the world.

The biggest problem seemed to be cooking his meals. The galley had a small two burner propane cook top and it was virtually impossible to find two pots small enough so that he could use them both at the same time on his tiny stove. There was also no counter space. The small sink had a little fiberglass cover which he used to prepare his meals on, but whenever he needed water, he would temporarily lose his counter space.

Apart from these minor inconveniences, he immensely enjoyed having his own space. Here, he could become himself again and could work on forgetting entirely this latest disastrous episode of his life.

He wasn't totally sure yet, that his work would necessarily only be just about forgetting. He knew he also needed to grow and learn from the experience, but could he learn to forgive her for the hurt and the injustice that he had suffered? He pondered this but found no immediate answers, yet he knew, that someday, somewhere deep inside of him he would find the answers he searched for.

Once his phone was installed, he phoned Michelle's

brother and her father. Both lived in Clearwater and he very much wanted to meet with them.

He had been thinking for some time now, that they might be able to help him to better understand why Michelle had acted in the way that she had. After all, they had known her more intimately and longer than anyone.

Eric had met Mark and his wife Annie several times. They had of course come to their wedding, but for some reason, he had never been able to warm up to them. Mark was the business manager for a Baptist church in Clearwater and Eric had originally hoped to be closer to him. He had thought that his ties with the church would make him a more conscious person, but he was, he discovered, totally wrong in that assessment.

When he phoned Mark at his home one night after eight, Annie told him that he was still at the office and she promised that Mark would phone him back as soon as he came in. Nothing else was said. Not, "How are you Eric?" no small talk of any kind, just this empty promise.

Eric waited till ten that evening and then decided to call again. This time, Mark answered the phone.

"Hello Mark," Eric said. "Sorry to call so late, but I didn't know if you got my message. I want very much to meet with you and your dad. I thought that the three of us could have a good heart to heart talk."

"I can't talk for my dad of course, but I am really not too interested in making the time available to talk to you Eric. This is a very busy time of the year for me. Perhaps we can talk on the phone. What is it you want to talk about?"

Eric was more than a little perplexed. He wondered what kind of person Mark was. How could he be so totally indifferent to helping him and Michelle in at least trying to mediate their terrible conflict? If he had known that she was mentally unstable, why would he or his father not try to convince Michelle to seek medical help?

He tried to say as much on the phone, but Mark did not want to go there at all.

"Eric," he said, "you are not of our faith. I said as much to Annie when we heard that you guys were planning to get married. I said to her then that this would never work out. I can pray for you guys of course, but that is about all. I am convinced that this marriage was wrong from the beginning. Give me your phone number where I can reach you and if I or my dad change our minds, we will give you a call."

Eric thought there was little point in continuing the conversation, so he left his number, said goodbye and hung up.

"These are not my family," he thought. He didn't know these people and he concluded that he didn't want to know them either.

His days went by pleasantly enough, working on his boat, reading and taking the time to try to resolve his inner conflicts and of course, meeting and talking to his fellow boaters.

Many of them lived on board year round he discovered and they had regular jobs. Usually, if he tried to shower early in the morning or late at night, those who worked would line up for their turns, so he learned to avoid these times.

The weather was turning unusually cold for Florida and often, Eric had problems falling asleep because he was so cold, even though he would put on additional layers of clothing. His boat was not equipped for living on board and it did not have a heating system.

He was afraid of buying a space heater because of the horror stories he had heard, but finally he succumbed. He spoke to one of his neighbors who told him that now they made them accident proof. He made a trip to Wal-Mart and bought a small unit and although there was no plug in the forward cabin where his bunk was, it did keep him much more comfortable.

Time heals everything and he began to think of her less and less.

Then one night out of the blue she called him. He figured she must have gotten his phone number from her brother or her dad.

She said that she was on her way traveling south on the interstate from Atlanta. She had stayed with Mitch, but they had a fight and so she had left there.

He thought, "Those actions sound familiar," but he didn't say so.

"I just wanted to tell you Eric that you are a bastard. I think you are despicable for having done this to me."

At first he thought she was drunk, but he knew she seldom drank. He wanted to ask her what he had done to her, but she wasn't about to give him an opening. She just kept on talking and she sounded hysterical.

"You are scum, and I am not surprised, you being a Jew and all. You are a coward as well for not admitting what you did to me."

She went on and on, spitting out one abuse after another. Now he understood where Mark got his opinions from, or was it the other way around? Michelle was after all his older sister. "We inherit our prejudices and then we wonder where our perceptions come from," he thought. "Can we really blame people for their false perceptions?"

He just let her rave and rant on. There wasn't any point

in trying to argue with her. She seemed so totally mad, so completely out of control.

Then she became quiet for a while and he noted a complete change in her. "There is no point for me to live on, Eric, life is useless and I cannot bear the hurt and the pains any longer. It is becoming too much for me. I tried to get closer to Christ, but even there I am a failure."

She tried to say some more things but she became vague and indefinable. The phone went dead. "She must have been using a telephone card," he thought. "She probably just used up her time."

Still, he was very concerned. She probably had called from a phone booth at one of the many rest stops on the interstate. He had wanted to tell her to go to a hospital and get some help, but of course she wouldn't have listened to him.

He sat there for a long time pondering in the dark cabin what he should do.

His thoughts finally took control of his usually rational mind and he phoned her dad.

"This is Eric," he said. "I am sorry to call you so late, but I just heard from Michelle. She seems so very distraught and I am afraid she might do something foolish. Have you heard from her? Can you call Mitch in Atlanta? Perhaps he knows where she was heading. Someone must track her down and reach her to tell her to go to a hospital and get some help."

"No Eric, I haven't heard from her," came the cool and aloof answer. "She phoned me from Atlanta and said she would spend a few days with Mitch. Then she planned to drive south, to spend Christmas here. If I hear something, I will let you know."

The line went dead. Eric tried to understand why the old man didn't want to talk further. It was late and he had probably been awakened by Eric's call. Besides, he remembered what Mark had said. Her entire family was probably biased, but he couldn't understand why her father had not been more concerned about his daughter's welfare.

"Better to leave it alone now," he thought. He had done what any concerned person would have done. It was out of his hands. He couldn't do anything further.

But he couldn't sleep. He was really worried about her and feeling powerless to do anything about it didn't help much.

He decided to read and he hoped that this distraction would calm his overactive mind enough to get some sleep.

He must have just dozed off but was immediately fully awake when the phone rang again.

"I am sorry Eric, to wake you in the middle of the night. I feel much better now. I am calmed down and I am no longer angry. I am sorry that you were made to feel the brunt of it. I drove to Tampa. I had planned to spend the night with my daughter and granddaughter, but her boyfriend was there and they weren't very nice to me. I guess I was still too angry to be understanding of how they felt about this intrusion. So I left there. I know where you are, Eric, I am not far away from you. Could you meet me at the Pier? Perhaps we can talk."

At first Eric was amazed at the change in her. She seemed so totally reasonable now. Then he wondered how on earth she knew where he was. He hadn't told anyone where his boat was docked, and in view of what had happened he didn't feel he wanted to meet with her.

"I called your dad, Michelle, I was worried about you. It is late and you need a place to stay. Why don't you call your parents? I am sure they will be happy to put you up. Or, go to a hotel. If you do not have the money, I will call the Hilton. You know where it is, it is really close to the Pier. I will make the reservations for you and have them charge it to my credit card."

"No Eric, you don't have to do that. Thanks for the offer, but I will be alright. I will call you tomorrow and perhaps we can meet and talk then. Good night Eric. Sleep with the angels."

The phone went dead before he had an opportunity to respond, or ask her where she planned to sleep.

Of course now he wouldn't be able to sleep at all. He looked at his watch. It was four in the morning. He decided to get dressed and walk over to take a shower. God, he was cold. He dressed quickly and of course he found the showers totally empty at that hour. To his surprise, the water was warmer than he had expected and he enjoyed standing there, letting the hot stream warm him thoroughly, as he thought about the occurrences of the previous night.

She was a very disturbed person, he thought, there was no question about that. But what now? Could he walk away from all of this and eventually get a divorce from her? Or did he have a responsibility of first trying to get her well?

After all, if the shoe would have been on the other foot, how would he have felt if she simply abandoned their marriage because he had become ill?

"In a way, *she* had done this," he thought. Were these not the actions of a person, who had wanted their marriage to end? Perhaps because he had been unable to give her the kind of sexual gratification that she wanted or needed? Wouldn't that kind of reasoning be the result of someone's thinking who has severe emotional problems, he wondered? Or was it just selfishness on her part?

If they were to remain together, he would have to make sure that she would get medical help. This could be a very lengthy and costly situation. She no longer had medical insurance either in the U.S. or in Canada and things like this could take years to get corrected, if ever. And then, there was always the question if she was willing to do what it took to get well. Would she cooperate?

Why was he now thinking this? Was he seriously considering in taking her back? Maybe not, but what about compassion? If the world was ever to become a better place, it would be because we would need to learn to become more compassionate and more tolerant. Should these same principals not also apply to his wife?

He decided not to look too far ahead. There was no point in thinking about the future. It was best, he thought, to just deal with the present moment and to be here for her if she needed his help.

He thought about going for a long walk. The exercise would do him good. Perhaps he would even see her, since she said she was close by and then they could talk.

He realized now that if he ever wanted to really meaningfully talk with her in the future, he would have to pick his times very carefully, when she was not in her fear mode. Fear, he realized, made people often do such stupid things and he understood well that when she was in her fear, she could not feel his love.

As he walked the empty streets, he began to see very faintly at first, this long night being chased away by the illumination of yet another day. Nothing was ever totally at rest. Creation had designed cycles. He was sure there were reasons for these cycles. Were the cycles in her mind so very different, that he couldn't learn to deal with these as well?

Chapter
THIRTEEN

She phoned him again around eight thirty. He had just finished scrubbing his decks and he was about to take another shower.

"Eric, I am going to mass at nine at St. Joseph's Church. I will be there till about ten. I believe they will close the doors at that time and I shall wait for you till then. If you are not there, I shall know that you are not coming. I do not know exactly where the church is. But I think it is on the corner of 11th Ave. South and 18th St. I am phoning you from a convenience store close to the church, or so I am told. This is the church where Father John preaches. I have heard him before and if I have a chance to meet with him, I am sure he can help me understand what has happened to us. I will look for you."

Eric knew roughly how far away the church was based on her directions. He had time to take a quick shower he decided and be there in plenty of time, in any case, well before ten.

He thought he found the convenience store where she said she had phoned from, but no one there seemed to know where the church was. He asked for a phone book and discovered that there were several St. Joseph's churches in the Bay area. One of them was in Clearwater and another in St. Petersburg, but that one was not on 11th Ave. South. It was instead on 11th Ave. North.

He raced up to the north end of town and arrived there just a little before ten, just as the caretaker was closing up the sanctuary. Michelle was nowhere to be found. He walked the streets in the vicinity of the church, hoping to find her car, while he thought about this latest strange occurrence. He didn't like to think this way, but what kind of a game was she playing?

He returned to his boat and waited impatiently for her next call.

"Isn't it strange," he thought. A few days ago he seemed quite content to keep her out of his life forever and now, he was actually waiting for her next call.

The next morning, he received a call from her about nine.

"Eric, I am in Tampa now. I have been staying at my parents' house, but they kept interfering with my whereabouts, always asking me where I was going and you know how I hate that. I have made up with my daughter and I am now staying here at her place in Tampa. There is an Episcopal Church close by. Can you meet me there so we can talk?"

Eric decided to first ask her about the last wild goose chase and explained that he had been there just around ten, because originally, he had gone to the wrong end of town but by the time he got there they were just closing up.

"Eric, I was there till well after ten. I waited till about ten-thirty and when you didn't show up, I left. I was quite disappointed that you didn't come."

Hadn't she been listening? Hadn't she heard what he just told her?

He decided that this was probably not a good time to get to the bottom of it. In due course he would find out what really happened. In the meantime, he would give her the benefit of the doubt.

He carefully wrote out the directions. She had said to meet him there Christmas Day, that would be tomorrow. Tonight was Christmas Eve. "There is a mass at eleven, and it will be over by noon."

He found the church without any problems, but it was shut tight. He walked around hoping to find her car. Then he spotted a side door and after he entered, found someone there who was cleaning the church. He asked the woman about the mass at eleven.

"No," she said. "That was yesterday. Today there will not be a mass at all."

Now he was totally confused. He was sure that she had told him Christmas Day. That was today. Was there a lesson in this? There probably was, he decided, but he couldn't figure it out. This was totally bizarre.

He went back to Final Draft and as he entered the office to check if he had any mail, he met one of his new friends, whose boat was docked at the other side of the Marina.

Jim often used the Captain's lounge upstairs to plug in his computer, so he could access the Net. Eric had met him there several times and they had gone out together a few times to have a beer. He'd also taken Jim to the Science of Mind Church in Clearwater, where he had been going every Sunday morning, since he had arrived back in Florida.

Jim seemed rather a lost soul, whose wife had divorced him totally out of the blue one day, or so he said, and Eric had thought that the friendly and loving atmosphere at that congregation, where the emphasis was on spirituality and not so much on religion, would be good for him.

"Hi Eric," Jim said as he entered the office. "Your wife was up here one night quite late. I was working up at the Captain's lounge doing some research work on the Net, and she came up to ask if I knew where your slip was. I gave her directions, but then, she did not seem to be too interested in going there after all. As I said, I was busy with some research project and I guess I wasn't very talkative or hospitable. She left suddenly without saying goodbye."

Later, Eric discovered that this was the night when she had called him twice and she had apparently slept in her car in the Marina parking lot across the street from there. He was appalled that she had thought it perfectly safe and sane to do so, but he knew better than to question her about that.

He was still perplexed how she had managed to find out where he was and he begun to wonder now, if she was stalking him. He had seen a movie a long time ago, about a woman stalking a man, he couldn't remember the name of it, but he remembered that the woman had tried to kill the guy's wife. The ending was when the guy finally had to kill the woman in self-defense. That woman had also been deranged and the guy hadn't found out about this until later in the movie.

Eric began to see how the mind can function in dangerous patterns and he realized how important it was for him to keep control over his perceptions. "I need to stay focused," he thought. "So much of what we do and how we act is caused by these perceptions, which program our minds, often in distorted ways."

When she called the next morning, he explained to her

as patiently as he could about their latest fiasco in trying to meet. "Why do we have to meet at a church?" he asked.

"Because Eric, it is the only place where I can feel safe with you."

He felt terribly hurt by what she had just said, not because she had said it, but because she so obviously believed it. He let out a deep sigh and said, "Ok. Where do you want to meet now? Can we please be sure this time that we both get it straight?"

He now began to see more clearly how her mind was afflicted if she really believed that he assaulted her.

"There is a noon Mass at St. Jude's hospital chapel. It is an easy place for you to get to from where you are."

She gave him directions and he asked her where he could reach her in the event that they would miss each other again. She told him that she did not feel safe in giving him that information. They hung up and Eric, feeling the hurt like a vice tightened around his chest and terrible frustrated, wanted to hurry now, so he would be sure to be there on time for the noon Mass. He changed quickly from his boating attire into a casual pair of trousers and tee shirt.

During the drive there, he felt hopeless and depressed. She really did believe that he was that kind of man, someone who in anger would assault a woman. As long as she saw him this way, how could he ever trust him again? Was he fighting impossible odds? Was all this an exercise in futility?

He was early and he spotted her in the front pew. She looked so petite and so very much at peace. "God, she is beautiful," he thought and all of his resoluteness and his depression melted like snowflakes in the early spring sun.

He sat down next to her, looked carefully into her eyes

but could not detect any fear. He took her small hand into his and they sat quietly like that until the Mass ended.

Everyone around them shook hands and hugged and it therefore felt very natural for him to take her into his arms as well. This was the first time in many months that they had embraced and they stood there for quite some time, silently and still, nor caring that people were leaving, not saying anything, just holding each other.

They parted only after they realized that the caretaker had entered to extinguish the mass candles and that everyone had left the small chapel. Only then, did he let her go, a little embarrassed.

What he felt at that moment was pure love. Unencumbered by his horrible memories. Not restricted by perceptions and unhindered by his egoist mind. At that very instant, he was able to forgive her for how he had suffered.

Could he discover a way so their lives together would always be like this? He realized that there were, what appeared to be, insurmountable problems and that he could only take responsibility to continue to work on his own stuff. To do his level best. It would be up to her to do her own repair work, that is, if she thought it was important enough and if she really loved him.

Over lunch he asked her what her plans were. Was she going back to Toronto, or was she planning to remain in Florida for a while longer?

"I do not know Eric; we have a lot of work to do. If I do go back to Toronto now, we cannot heal what needs to be healed, in the event that we decide to remain together. The court in Toronto decided that we should see a qualified councilor. We could possibly find someone here and see if together we can work on our problems."

Eric thought about this and then he said, "Michelle, where would you stay during the time that we have counseling? This is not the kind of thing that we can hope to resolve in a few weeks. Have you a place where you can stay?"

"I can stay a few days at a time with my parents and a few days at my daughter's, but Eric, couldn't I stay with you on your boat? I would prefer this."

Eric sat in silence for a while and then said, "Michelle, I have been thinking about renting an apartment for some time now. The boat is getting too confining for me, besides, it gets awfully cold at night, living on board. If it is too small for one, I can imagine what it would be like for the two of us. Not a terribly good place for us to do our work. I believe it would seriously hinder our chances. Let me find a two bedroom apartment. You would be able to have your privacy and it does give us a change to do our work together. I think, for it to be successful, we cannot do this work apart from each other, since a lot of the work we need to do has to do with our interactions."

"Ok Eric," she said. "That sounds like a good plan. It is getting close to the New Year; perhaps I can stay on the boat for a few days while we look for an apartment starting the beginning of January. This will also give us a little time to ask some of our friends if they can recommend a therapist who can work with us."

They parted. She, to collect her things and he, about twenty feet off the ground, to drive back to Final Draft and to make room for her in the second cabin, which up to now, he had used mostly for storage.

He remembered that they had taken a series of ballroom-dancing lessons before their marriage. Now, that seemed like such a long time ago. So much had happened since then. He knew she loved to dance. A few weeks ago, he had heard of a New Year's Eve party and he and some of his friends had planned to go there, although at that time there had not been much for him to celebrate. He stopped over at the Old Casino Ballroom on his way home to pick up another ticket for her. He knew she would be pleasantly surprised and when he told her about the dance, she threw her arms around him and hugged him like a little girl who had just received the most beautiful doll in the world.

They both dressed up for the occasion but just as they planned to leave for the dance, it started to rain. It was one of those horrendous downpours that Florida is famous for. They had quite a distance to walk to his car and he decided to call some of his friends to see if they still planned to go.

One of them suggested that they should dress in his foul weather gear which Eric always kept on board in case he ran into some bad storms.

They advised, "You could always carry your dress-up clothing in a plastic bag to keep them dry and you can change in the washrooms."

As they rushed to his car, they giggled and laughed like little kids, while they ran in their sandals trough ankle-deep puddles of streaming water.

He dropped her off in front of the ballroom and then went to park his car. He felt lightheaded and carefree. He was happier than he could remember being for a long while. He didn't care if it would continue to rain all night long. He liked the sound of the water splashing underneath his rubber sandals and the noise that the falling rain made as it bounced heavily off the palm leaves overhead.

"This is so weird," he thought, "these highs and lows in

my life." He had never had to deal with this before his marriage to her, then his life had been fairly constant. He wondered if this might be a byproduct of being in love.

He spotted her as he was leaving the men's room, after he had dried off and changed. She looked stunning and ravishing to him. Far too young and too beautiful to be fifty-six years old, he thought.

He liked it when she complimented him. "Eric, we were just talking about you. Everyone agrees that you look like a younger version of Richard Gere."

"Younger?" he said. "You mean older?" She laughed.

They danced almost every dance and when the band announced the countdown to bring in the New Year, he kissed her gently. He had not been kissed so passionately in public before. Her arms went around his neck and she squeezed him so tight that he wondered where such a petite person got all her strength from.

When they left to return to Final Draft, the rain had stopped and the big puddles had all but disappeared. They walked hand in hand over the break-water to his slip. The view over the bay was superb with tiny sparkling lights everywhere reflecting on the bay waters. The sky was clear now. There was a fresh breeze blowing from the west and it had turned into one of those beautiful balmy nights that Florida is so well known for. Stars twinkled brightly overhead and Eric almost managed to convince himself that all of this surely was an omen of many good things yet to come.

He was careful however not to make love to her. He wanted to very much, but he thought it would be destructive to the rebuilding of their relationship and he wished fervently that she wouldn't feel disillusioned.

They had planned for some of his friends to visit them

on Final Draft at noon the following day for a glass of champagne to help toast in the New Year and Eric was much
looking forward to this little get-together. He fell asleep
thinking of how fortunate he was to feel so loved. "Like
walking in on a party unexpectedly and being embraced by
everyone there just for coming to join them." It was a good
feeling.

New Year's Day was picture postcard gorgeous. The sky
was this unbelievable blue color, which even the splendor of
nature or alternatively, a very talented painter could not have
improved upon. There was a cool breeze and absolutely no
humidity.

They discussed the latest atrocity of a human bomb blast
at a busy market in Israel and Eric's friend John, who had
lived in Israel for a few years, got into a heated discussion
with Michelle about the benefits of religion.

There seemed to be no stopping her when John, who
had a Catholic upbringing, voiced an opinion that he
thought religion had been largely responsible for so many
deaths and that humanity hadn't learned a damn thing ever
since the Crusades and we were still doing our stupid bit in
ethnic cleansing.

At one point, Michelle became very hostile with him
because he did not agree with her and she became very
adamant about her own point of view.

No one wanted to stay much longer after that. Everyone
seemed a little bit embarrassed about Michelle's antagonism
and found some lame excuse to leave because of other commitments.

After they had all gone, Eric said, "Michelle, why did you
have to become so angry with John about his point of view?
Were you aware that you were talking almost constantly and

that you would not allow anyone else to voice their opinions? As usual, you were hogging the conversation Michelle."

He knew, he should have been more careful in the way he put that. He was instantly aware that he had been accusatory and judgmental. "But God," he thought, "I am not perfect. I do make mistakes, if I was perfect, I wouldn't learn anything. We only learn from our mistakes. If I have to pussy foot around all the time about what I say and how I say it, how can I be myself?"

She turned on him like an angry cat. "You are always 'you-ing' me to death Eric. I am tired of always having to defend myself with you. I knew that this wasn't going to work out. I knew there was going to be trouble the moment you brought out the champagne. My father also drank too much and he made us miserable."

"Michelle," Eric pleaded, "everyone had one small paper cup of champagne. I don't exactly call this a drinking problem. Why do you always have to change the circumstances? Or exaggerate them. Blow everything out of proportion, why do you? That is simply not honest."

"Oh, so now I am dishonest too. I am not going to remain here and put up with these insults."

She went down below, got her things together and angrily walked off Final Draft.

Initially he wanted to stop her and try to reason with her, but then he thought, What was the point? This was never going to work out between them.

If she did not get her way, the world was coming to an end. He decided, he could not live with her like that. Could her outburst have been avoided, if he had apologized, he wondered?

At first, he thought that she might turn back, after she

had an opportunity to reflect on everything. He looked at her as she walked across the breakers. Her small but elegant body an expression of sheer anger, her sandaled feet stubbornly hitting the concrete more brutally than was necessary. She never looked back and a few instants later she was out of his line of sight.

He thought about her a lot that day. Should he call her? Where? He had no idea where she had gone.

Perhaps he had been too direct with her. He could have voiced his concerns a little different! He should have found a way to put it less critical.

As the day progressed he once again began to feel how hopeless things were between them and he wished that she had not found him when she did. He had just then been getting used to life without her.

Chapter
FOURTEEN

She phoned him three days later. He had been busy looking for an apartment, which proved to be more difficult than he had first thought. It was getting close to high season in Florida and anything that was remotely close to the beaches had been booked long ago.

He finally found a pleasant apartment in a wooded area overlooking a small lake. It was close to where he had lived before, when he had been married to Jane. He was comfortably familiar with the area and the shopping in the vicinity but he could only rent it for the month of January. However nothing else was available but a two bedroom suite.

He rented it and hoped that he might find something else for the remainder of the season. "I could always spend the time traveling," he thought, "in the event that I can't find anything. Or, when it gets warmer, I could move back to my boat."

He doubted though, that he wouldn't be able to find what he wanted, if he would spend a little more time looking. "It might be a little pricier, but I really do not want to live on board any longer." It had been okay for a short while and he felt he had learned and grown a lot from the experience, but enough was enough, he decided.

He didn't have a lot of things to move and it didn't take him very long to get his things into the apartment. "That is the good thing about letting go of possessions," he thought. "Less things to worry about."

He had canceled his phone on his boat, since the apartment already had a phone and he phoned Michelle's dad to give him his new number in case she wanted to get in touch with him.

He loved being in his new place, even though it would only be for a month. It was such a difference from living on board. Here, he had the space to cook proper meals, he could stretch out on a comfortable chair and read and the thing he loved most of all, he was to be able to take a hot shower whenever he felt like it without having to line up. Having a long hot shower he now considered a real luxury.

"Funny," he thought, "how easily we take all the simple things in life for granted until they are no longer available to us."

Finally, he was able to live once again in the more comfortable lifestyle which he had been accustomed to and which he had missed so much during the time that he had not been allowed to go back to his own home.

Then, one morning, just as he had finished his meditation, she called.

"Good morning Eric. I have been staying at St. Leo's Abbey in Lakeland. It is a small monastery and retreat house. It has been inexpensive for me to remain here, while I tried to figure things out. I am planning to return to Toronto later this afternoon or tomorrow and perhaps we can talk before I leave. Would you like to drive out here? It is really a lovely place. There is a nice lake, it is very scenic and secluded and we could sit and talk without pressures. You know, Eric, I always feel so much better whenever I am close to nature."

He thought about what she had said. He had missed her very much, he knew, and he did need to talk to her some more about their problems. Too many things had remained unsaid. This would perhaps be the only opportunity for them to talk before she left. In Toronto, he would not be allowed to talk to her and he felt that, based on how she sounded, this would probably be a good time to reach out to her.

She gave him directions on how to get there and he quickly dressed. It would be about an hour's drive, she had said and if she was to leave this same afternoon to start driving back, she did not want to leave too late.

As he drove up to the guest parking area, he spotted her. Petite, and elegantly clad in a plain, cool looking little printed cotton dress. His favorite.

Even in an ordinary dress such as this, she has the ability to look great, he decided.

She walked over to where he had parked his car and as he got out, she kissed him lightly on his cheek. He smelled her: a blend of freshly washed hair and the scent of her aromatic oils which she preferred using instead of perfumes.

He stood there, holding her, not wanting to let go; the feel of their bodies touching and her smell.

She wanted him to see the chapel, the grounds and the cottage where she had lived for the past several days. They held hands as she excitedly showed him around. They found a small bench near the lake and they talked. He knew then, deep down, that he couldn't let her go.

She talked to him again about them seeking counseling. The ideas she suggested were similar to their previous discussions but this time she had the name of a psychotherapist which had been highly recommended by one of her friends.

As they sat there, in the warm sunshine, looking at the shimmering lake and listening to the multitude of birds singing their love songs to one another, he couldn't help but dream about the possibility of finding some way to solve their problems.

"Would it really be possible," he thought, "for therapy to make our being together a lasting reality?" How wonderful that would be, if they could finally be in a peaceful and loving relationship, something he had wanted so much for so long, but which had always seemed to be evasive to him.

He told her then about the two bedroom apartment he had moved into and suggested that since there was this extra bedroom, it would be a good place for them to live during their therapy sessions.

The bells of the chapel chimed in the distance and Michelle wanted them to go to the noon Mass. They quickly walked back and took their seats just as Mass was about to begin. Eric wondered silently what it was that brought forth within her this need to be comforted in churches. These seemed to have been her favorite places at times of much confusion in her life.

Then, he let that thought go as unworthy and judgmental. "If she needed this in order to be his loving bride," he thought, "so be it. She should be entitled to find the strength she needed in any place and however she needed to." He had read somewhere that the chemical imbalances which caused depressions could be controlled through deep prayers, which altered this mental state. Whatever it took, he thought, "I am prepared to live with it."

After a simple lunch in the Abbey's little eating space

reserved for guests, they drove back to the Bay area, she, following him closely behind in her own car.

He was pleased when she complimented him on his find and he proudly guided her around the small but cozy apartment. He showed her where her room and bathroom were located and she began to unpack her things.

They both agreed that it was best, in the beginning at least, to see two different psychotherapists. This way they could compare notes and they could decide which one would be their favorite choice when they would be ready to have their sessions together.

She was still convinced that he had choked her and he thought it best, for the time being, not to argue with her about what had occurred that night.

When that following morning, he met with Sandy, the psychotherapist he had selected, he immediately took a liking to her. She was a very large woman and her intelligent eyes were soft velvety brown. Her natural red hair was shoulder length, parted in the center and severely pulled back from her face, which at first seemed like a contradiction to her soft and very feminine features. She wore long flowing supple and comfortable looking garments, which she occasionally and lovingly gathered around her. She sat partially reclined in a comfortable and overstuffed loveseat and she invited Eric to sit opposite her in an equally relaxing looking leather chair.

She seemed very sensitive to their issues and was a careful and attentive listener.

Before he left her plant filled office that day, he decided that he must ask her about something that had been troubling him for some time now.

"How is it possible Sandy," he said, "that two reasonably

intelligent people can see the truth of what happened that night so completely different? Is Michelle making all this up for reasons I would not like to assume?"

"It is entirely possible Eric, that Michelle could have had a traumatic experience, either during or even before childbirth or when she was a little girl, growing up. It could have been caused by a caregiver whom she had fully trusted and who had violated that trust. She may have been so very hurt by this, that she has locked it away in her mind. Then, this fear could come up suddenly, whenever she feels very threatened and she would be reliving this horrible experience all over again, causing her to remember it so vividly at that very instant, seeing her previous agony of the aggressor replayed in her mind, making anyone responsible whom she trusted and whom she felt threatened by. Alternatively Eric, something in your own childhood could have created such fear, that it would make you unknowingly strike out against the intruder without remembering the entire incident later on."

Eric was stunned. Neither possibility had ever occurred to him. He doubted that he could ever unknowingly choke his wife. It was possible of course, but he thought he knew himself well enough to eliminate this possibility altogether. He would not be capable of doing this kind of thing, no matter how badly he would have been hurt in his childhood. He just knew that much about himself.

It did explain a lot about Michelle's actions and tears welled up in his eyes when he thought of her agony. Her apparent greediness for demanding half of his house, could have been caused by her severe insecurity, which could well be part of that very condition which also caused her extreme fears and anxiety.

On his way home, he decided not to say anything about

his discoveries. There would be no point to it. If she did not remember why she had acted that way, she most certainly would not remember it now. It might make matters worse. "Best to leave that kind of stuff to the professionals," he thought.

When he returned to the apartment, she was already there. She had liked John she said, the therapist she had gone to.

After he told her about Sandy, she said, "Eric, perhaps we can make an appointment to see John together and then we could see Sandy as a couple. We should be able to make a better decision after that, to decide which one of them we will select in the end."

He agreed. "That's a good idea, Michelle, let's make the appointments right away and see them both as soon as possible." He was convinced that what they were doing was right and he wanted to move things along as quickly as possible.

He was also keenly aware of observing his lifelong flaws of becoming too impatient about things and he wanted to keep control over this anxiousness. "This is odd," he thought. He had never before been able to look at his shortcomings in quite the same way. Like a kindly stranger looking at his thoughts. Perhaps, not exactly like a stranger but more like his other self.

They did see John together the following evening.

Eric liked him right from the start, but he said to Michelle after their appointment, "I do think a woman might be able to be a little more sensitive to our problems. We have an appointment with Sandy later this week. I hope you will like her as much as I do. We can then make our decision."

He hoped that he wasn't steering Michelle towards

Sandy, solely because of what Sandy had shared with him. He hadn't meant to do that. He wanted to remain as transparent as possible and let her make her own decisions. What Sandy had shared was critically important, of course, and might help to give them both a better understanding of what had really taken place that night, but he shouldn't try to manipulate Michelle. Instead, he should allow her to make an independent decision based on her own choices.

"Eric," she told him after their appointment, "I really like Sandy a lot. But I would like to have an appointment with her by myself, without you. Is that all right? And then we can make our decision."

On the morning of her appointment he was a little nervous. He wondered what they might be talking about. He knew this was foolish of course. He should learn to let things happen as they were intended to, but nevertheless he paced the apartment nervously while she was out.

He was working it up, he knew. "What's wrong with me?" he thought. "Why am I not able to control my thoughts? Why is my mind taking over here?

"It feels good to know that I am present enough to observe this," he reasoned, "for as long as I see it, I am aware of what I am doing and I know it is not in my best interest to be this way. This is not my highest."

When Michelle returned, he was quietly reading. He looked up at her closely though, when she entered the apartment to see if he could detect something from the expression on her face, but she seemed very relaxed and happy and he did not push her for information.

He wanted her to tell him about her appointment in her own good time and he was quite proud of himself. The old Eric would have wanted a full accounting the moment she returned. He was learning, he decided, to stop taking control. Something that was left over from his business days, but not a very useful skill in learning how to become more of a loving person in relationships.

Later that afternoon, she seemed pleased to want to talk about her appointment. She was very excited, she said, about the prospects of working through their problems with Sandy and she was full of hope.

Eric hugged her passionately and said, "You know honey, I was sort of hoping you would say that, but I tried very hard not to influence you. I too am excited about working with her." Then, he remembered and apologized for his forgetfulness of calling her "honey."

Their first appointment with Sandy did not go well however. Michelle kept interrupting him whenever he wanted to share some of his feelings.

He was a little surprised that Sandy did not take more control over what was happening. Then, he began to relax. He stopped worrying about the amount of money Michelle's interruptions were costing him. Surely, Sandy knew what she was doing. It did give her an opportunity, he decided, to experience Michelle, in a way that she would not have otherwise.

At their next appointment tough, he mentioned to Sandy that they should have some sort of rule.

He didn't like the way that came out.

He immediately corrected himself. "Perhaps we should not try to talk both at the same time. Could we divide up the hour? In this way, I can say what I feel I need to for the first half and Michelle can then take up the remaining time?"

They agreed, but Michelle still interrupted occasionally.

On each subsequent visit they were making some progress, but it was hard to tell where they were heading, until Sandy made an observation which made so much sense, that Eric thought it was a wonder that they themselves hadn't thought about it before.

"The thing that stands out like a sore thumb and seems to be most in the way for enabling you to be together in a happy relationship is the lack of trust you both have. Michelle, you must realize that if you wish to monetarily benefit from the house in Toronto, your marriage is over. So if the house in Toronto was no longer an issue, then that could eliminate a lot of distrust for both of you. The only thing then left for you to deal with is the differences by which you both view what really happened on that night when Eric was arrested."

At this point, Sandy shared with Michelle the same information she had told Eric on his first visit there, about the possibility of a traumatic experience suffered by either of them as young children.

Since this all came up toward the end of their fifth appointment and they were both dealing with a great deal of emotional energy at that time, Sandy suggested that they end their session earlier than usual.

On their drive home that evening, they were both quiet and very much in their own thoughts. Eric had some ideas he wanted to run by Michelle, but he intuitively knew that the timing wasn't right.

For the first time in many weeks, he wasn't as optimistic as he had been before, but he did not know why, nor did he know where this feeling was coming from.

Michelle also seemed to be upset about something. He thought that it might have something to do with what Sandy had shared with her at the end of their visit. He himself was feeling a little gloomy as well, but he couldn't tell if his feelings were related to Michelle's state of mind. He did realize that her mood swings affected him deeply.

"Michelle," he said to her after breakfast the next morning, "Sandy feels that a lot of the stress and the pressures that we are experiencing, are due to the loss of trust because you seem to think that you are entitled to have half of my house in Toronto. Yet you have told me many times that you really do not like to live there. You told me repeatedly that if you had a choice, you would prefer to live in Hendersonville, N.C. Why don't we buy a house there together? You must have most of your money left from the sale of your house in Florida. We would split everything right down the middle. I don't know yet what we want to do about the furniture we have in Toronto. We might want to begin all over, buying everything new. Make a fresh start so to speak.

"I do however have one condition, and that is that you relinquish your claim on the house in Toronto. I don't want you to give me your answer now. I want you to think about this very carefully before you decide. Our rental time for the apartment here runs out in a couple of days. We would have to start looking for something else, should we decide to remain here and continue on with Sandy. If you decide that you like the idea of going to North Carolina, then we could go there at the end of the month, when our lease runs out here. We could rent something there and this would give me also an opportunity to see how I like it. I have not been there for any length of time and before we buy a house together, I would want to spend at least a month getting the feel of the place.

"Our counseling sessions with Sandy could not continue, should we decide to go to N.C. We would in that case be better off to find someone locally there."

She hadn't interrupted him. Not even once, which was unusual, considering the amount of information he had shared with her. He waited for her, to see if she had any questions, but apparently there were none. Not at least then.

"It is such a beautiful day," he said. "Why don't we clean away the breakfast dishes and go for a nice long walk on Honeymoon Beach? It is only a short distance from here and the fresh sea breezes will do us both good. It will give you a chance to think about what I have said. What do you say Michelle?"

Her mood seemed to change noticeably and she began to whistle softly, while she skipped to her bedroom to change into her bathing suit and shorts. She often whistled whenever she was in a good mood, he knew.

"She seems outrageously happy for someone who has so much thinking to do," he thought. Perhaps this was a good sign or, it was her way to deal with stress.

They walked hand in hand, barefooted through the sand warmed by the early morning sun. He loved her he knew. He loved her like the sound of the surf, the crying of the seagulls overhead and the windy smell of the salty air in his nostrils.

He must find some way to dispel all the hurts and the pain they had both suffered these past few months.

Chapter
FIFTEEN

He had bought a pair of short-wave radios the day before they left. The range was just one mile, but it was fine, he thought, as long as they remained pretty close together. They had decided to drive both cars, in the event that they made a decision to buy a house in Hendersonville, and Eric thought that the radios would be useful in helping them to communicate while driving to their destination. Michelle could then leave her car in the garage of their new home and together, they could drive up to Toronto in Eric's car.

"Michelle," Eric had said to her before they left, "it is of course entirely up to you to drive to Toronto with me. I will need to go, because Jamie has an important skating competition early in March and I promised to be there."

Driving up to Hendersonville and using the short-wave radios turned out to be a lot of fun. They talked often using this intercom system and mealtimes became a time to relax and to be together.

Sometimes, when Eric went a little too fast, he would lose contact with her as their radios only had a short range. He would then slow down until she answered his page with,

"Slow down, slow down my knight in shining armor, your wench is having a tough time keeping up with you."

He would let her pass then and to let her know that he got her message, he would salute her by raising his hand to his forehead in military fashion.

The next morning they rented a sweet little cottage for the entire month. It was located just a short distance from town and one might say that it had a very woodsy feeling to it. Even the cute little kitchen had pine wood paneling and the cathedral ceiling of their small bedroom was also made of pine wood.

Their cottage had one bedroom and their small bed was only just a twin size, which barely fitted into the room, but since the nights were quite cold, they often cuddled together to keep warm.

Eric had thought about this before he rented the cottage, as he was not accustomed to sleeping so close together, but he concluded that all the hype about queen or king size beds were really a hindrance to marital relationships. At least with a twin bed, if you had a disagreement, you could not avoid having to touch each other occasionally and often, that in itself could break down huge barriers.

Their bed in Toronto was king size with lots of room to escape to your own side. In his previous marriages he had always had either a queen or a king size bed. Perhaps that might have been part of his problems. But without having compassion, understanding and yes, love, this kind of logic was badly flawed, he concluded.

Nevertheless, in their new home, if there was to be one, he decided, he would prefer to have a twin bed. Neither of them were large people and they fitted well enough in this smaller and cozier size.

They hadn't slept together as husband and wife since Eric's arrest in October. He was well past the age when he would be easily aroused and especially since the massive radiation, he often had troubles keeping an erection for long. Orgasms of course had become mere memories since his illness.

Michelle on the other hand, being seventeen years his junior, wanted a healthy sex life and Eric very much wanted to please her. Every time he was capable in doing so, he felt grateful that he had been able to give her these gifts as an expression of his love, but this hadn't always been easy for him. Try as he would, Michelle was sometimes disappointed or frustrated.

He had tried Viagra of course, but it gave him headaches and it often would upset his stomach. Besides, he had to plan to take the little blue pill a few hours before it would work, and he didn't know how to ask her. He was a little embarrassed by the artificiality of it all.

Often, after he had taken the pill, she would not be interested any longer, or she had fallen asleep by the time the pill began to work for him. He would then needlessly suffer the consequences of the after effects, without having been able to give her what he knew would have given her pleasure.

Sometimes, he thought he was able to gauge her signals by the way she looked at him, but then, just to make doubly sure, he would ask her if he should take the pill. He did not want to take it without a valid reason. She would often reply affirmatively only to go to sleep angry. He never could figure out why.

Was she upset with him, he wondered, because he was not able to be more sexually spontaneous? But she knew all of this before she had agreed to marry him. He had kept nothing from her.

She had told him that her ex-husband had not been fertile and they had therefore decided to adopt. She had explained to Eric, that she had resented his infertility a lot, because he had not shared this with her before the marriage and she had been robbed of that wonderful experience, which most women have from childbirth.

Could she now be resentful, he wondered, that he was not like most men any longer, unable to give her what she wanted, when she wanted it?

Eric had tried to talk to her about this, but whenever he broached the subject of their sexuality, she would clam up and simply change the subject.

"Michelle," he had said to her one morning when she seemed particularly disappointed, "I think loving someone does not always need to be expressed by having intercourse. I think it is entirely possible to enjoy closeness often without me being inside you. Kissing and caressing also expresses how I feel about you. Just by being close together and the way we treat each other respectfully is one of the many ways that we can express our love for one another. Sometimes it is expressed by just the way I look at you and sometimes you express it to me by accepting my disability and showing me that you love me in spite of it."

She had run from the room then, sobbing and he had never wanted to talk about their sexuality again with quite the same frankness as he had done that morning. He felt he had exposed all of his vulnerability to her. He had been totally transparent and she had thrown it back in his face he felt, in a very uncaring way.

He knew of course she was hurting and perhaps someday, when she trusted him more, she would tell him what was really going on with her. How could she trust him fully now, when she was convinced that he had tried to choke her that night?

That first night, in that small double bed, sleeping so close together with their bodies touching, after so many months, he wanted so very much to make love to her and to give her all his preciousness, but it didn't work.

He kept on remembering how he had been arrested that night in October and he kept thinking, "Even if she believed that I tried to hurt her, how could she, if she really loved me, have me arrested? What kind of woman would do this?" But he had been unable to understand her fears! If only he could have known what had gone on in her mind, he would have been able to be more compassionate and there would have been trust and understanding between them.

He had been awake that first night for many hours thinking about this and he finally, before sleep overtook him, concluded that she must have had horrible fears in order to do what she did. Could he ever learn to forgive her for that, over which she had so little control? Or for that matter, could she ever forgive him? Could their relationship ever be fully healed?

He hoped that by buying a house in a place where she had always wanted to live and by selling his house in Toronto after less than a year there, it would prove to her once and for all how much he cared for her, how much he was willing to do for her and perhaps that might be enough to heal both of them. He prayed that it would.

Michelle thought that the best way for him to learn about Hendersonville, was to start looking at real estate. They contacted several real estate brokers and finally settled on a man who seemed to be most compatible with both of them.

They spent almost three weeks looking at many different

houses, but they kept coming back to one place in particular. It was set in a hilly area on several acres of land. A creek ran by the house and divided their property from the next lot. It had almost everything that they had put on their list of desirables, including a beautifully screened in veranda and sundeck and lots of wooded trails and nature. He knew she could be happy here. There was however a lot of grass to cut and they would have to get a motorized mower. Eric began to see himself as country squire and he liked that feeling. He too, could learn to love this place. The house was brand new and the small builder who guaranteed everything, lived close by just in case they ran into any problems.

Finally, they told the agent that they would need the weekend to really talk about it and that they would let him know by Monday.

"There isn't much else to see in any case," the agent had said. "You have pretty well seen it all."

Eric was pleased with the place. He didn't know much about country living, but he was sure he could learn whatever there was to learn in a relatively short time. He knew Michelle loved it very much and he hoped that this house might be the very thing that would heal them both.

On Sunday, Michelle said that she had pretty much decided. "You know Eric, we can have my granddaughter come visit with us in the summers and she would have a great time. She would love it out here, and it would expose her to a totally different kind of lifestyle. I really think it would do her a lot of good to get out of the Tampa Bay area once in a while."

"Michelle, I too like it very much out here. At first, I did not think that I would like to live in a small town. But here, I can visit a lawyer, the bank and do grocery shopping all in a few hours. In Toronto, the parking alone is a hassle, let alone the time that it takes to get from one place to the next. The people here are all very friendly and I can drive to Toronto whenever I want to see Jamie. It is only about a day's drive and if you wanted to see your family in the Tampa Bay area it is about the same distance. We are about halfway between the two places so also from that point of view, I have no hesitation."

"There is however one thing I want to make again very clear to you. If we buy this place, you will need to sign off on the house in Toronto. I am saying this to you once again, so there can be no misunderstandings later on. I am trusting you completely and I will agree to buy this place even before you sign off on the other house. I just want it to be clearly understood."

"I know Eric, and I already had agreed to this condition. I hope that we can in time forget about what happened between us and that we can now begin in earnest to trust each other and to start working on creating happiness in our marriage."

Eric was elated and they celebrated their decision by going out to dinner to one of the nearby country inns. Finally, he thought, they would begin the process of working towards becoming lovers again. He had learned the hard way that life is a process and each day he intended to weave a small fiber of his love into a strong and meaningful tapestry.

They phoned the real estate broker the following morning and both of them were elated to discover that since this would be a cash deal, they would be able to close on their purchase before going to Toronto at the end of the month.

Michelle had decided to travel with him. "We have a lot of packing to do if we intend to move to our new home by the end of April. I want to be back here in time to plant our vegetable garden," she said.

They told each other how much they liked how they felt about themselves and about each other. The elimination of fear for both Eric and Michelle and the regaining of trust, had done much to open their hearts to their outside world as well. They were able to now embrace it with joy and smiles and they knew intuitively that because of the way they sparkled, the world shined back at them.

They left early in the morning and the first half of their trip was quite different from the way they had traveled together before. They laughed a lot, had interesting discussions about countless topics and listened to their favorite music on Eric's superb sound system. He thought about this later and he had a hard time explaining to himself how their being together was so different this time. It was something he felt inside his body. There was a feeling somewhere between his stomach and his heart which fluttered and seemed to expand. He didn't want to explain this to Michelle, because he thought he might not be able to express it just right, but he knew instinctively that the God of his understanding was delighted about this new opportunity for their greater consciousness.

Just outside of Pittsburgh, Jane phoned Eric on his cell phone. After their usual polite chit chat, she came directly to the point. "Eric, I know that you are planning to come to Jamie's skating competition this weekend. She has not been skating well and I think that she is worried that you are bringing Michelle to see her compete. You know how your daughter is. As usual she finds it difficult to talk to you about this herself. She does not understand why you are back together again after Michelle had you arrested and I believe that she is worried about you. She does not know that I am calling you, so please don't tell her, but I think she would prefer it if you would come alone. Perhaps you yourself can talk to Jamie about it, but please don't tell her about our conversation," she repeated. "Just ask her how she would feel if you brought Michelle to the competitions."

At first, Eric didn't want to tell Michelle about the conversation he had with Jane. He deliberated about this for a while. He hadn't wanted to disrupt the closeness between them, but he decided that he did need to explain this to her. He might as well do it now, while they were driving, but he was concerned about how he should tell her and also how she would react to it.

"Michelle, that was Jane who just called."

"I know Eric, I have ears you know," she replied not too kindly.

"She wanted to know if you were coming to see Jamie compete. Were you planning to come?"

He very much hoped she would say no, so he could spare her the rest of Jane's telephone call.

"I don't know Eric, why is she asking? Jamie is the one competing, or is your ex-wife also a figure skater?" she asked a trifle sarcastically. "Is she trying to get back with you? Is that what this is all about?"

He knew then that she was back in her fear mode.

"No, of course not," and he had no choice now but to tell her about the rest of the conversation.

They talked for a while about the merits of allowing Jamie to decide if he should bring Michelle, but that magical connection they had before the telephone call had disappeared totally.

"I think that I will talk to Jamie personally, but if she

indeed does not want you to come, if she insists on getting her way in this, then I intend to tell her that I will not be able to come either. I think it is wrong to give a young child that kind of power. We are married and we are trying to make a renewed go of our marriage. I think Jamie is old enough to know that and sometimes things can go wrong between two people, but when they earnestly try to correct their problems, this is a positive thing for her to learn and family and friends should support us in our effort. I am sure that this is a good thing for her to understand."

For the balance of the trip and all the way to their house however, they talked very little, each of them with their own thoughts.

Eric could understand that Michelle was upset about the call. He hoped that when she came home, giving her a little time, she would be able to make allowances and accept the fact that there are many different ways to look at this. What is reality, he wondered? It so much depends on one's perceptions.

He understood that her past conditioning had made her fearful about their future together and that her old angsts were coming up. He needed to be understanding and patient with her. In time, and he was sure of this, they would be able to overcome this as well. They had come so far already.

That night, she went to bed angry. The first time she had been that way in a long while. "Welcome home Eric," he thought. He kissed her lightly on her cheek and he turned to his side of their massive king size bed. Too bad, that they did not have that small twin bed, because then, neither of them would have the opportunity to escape touching, and by doing so, they would feel this need for each other at times when the going gets a little tough. They would be able to feel each other's closeness and somehow he thought, then their souls could touch.

He was tired from the long drive home, but he slept the sleep of a troubled mind.

The next day was Friday and he had promised to take Jamie out for dinner that night. He spoke to her then about his responsibilities to both her and to Michelle his wife, and he asked for her help in resolving this uncomfortable situation.

He was more than a little surprised when Jamie said, "Dad, I have no problem whatsoever if Michelle wants to come and see me skate."

Eric thought it was best not to ask her why she had not been skating well that last week. He thought that this may have been something that Jane had perceived on her own, or perhaps Jamie may have told her mom this in order to feel more loved by her.

"What we don't do for love," he thought.

When he returned home later that night, he told Michelle what Jamie had said. "I am so glad she feels this way, Michelle. I would have felt awful to have missed seeing her compete. I am not going to try to figure it all out. The most important thing is that the issue has resolved itself. It is still entirely up to you if you want to come with me tomorrow to the competitions. I would like it of course if you would. As long as you know that I do not want you to feel obligated in any way."

"Of course I will go, Eric," she said, but he knew that she still carried some of her resentments.

Jamie did wonderfully well in the competitions. She came in first place with her artistic program. She had told

Eric that she had designed her own costume and she had done her own choreography.

Her program brought tears to his eyes and sent shivers down his back. This was his little girl, skating her heart out. He remembered well, when she had first started to skate at one of the malls in Clearwater. How clumsy she had been then, falling all over the place.

"Even back then," he thought, "when she began to get her balance and started to really skate, she showed a natural grace, which seemed to have been absent with many of the other children."

And here she was, at age thirteen winning this important competition.

The only thing missing for him, he thought, was that no one seemed to know that he was her father. Everyone was so busy congratulating Jane, but then, he corrected his thoughts—only he needed to have that knowledge.

Chapter SIXTEEN

The following Monday, Eric called his lawyer to tell him that Michelle had decided to sign off on the townhouse. He was told that Michelle needed to see her own lawyer first, before she could sign the de-registration papers for the deed. His lawyer promised to call him back after he had made an appointment with a lawyer for Michelle, which for convenience's sake was located in the same building.

He phoned Eric an hour or so later and said, "Eric, I have made an appointment for both of you to see me Wednesday morning at ten. Michelle's appointment with her lawyer should only take about ten minutes. After that, you can both come to my office to sign and then I can do the balance of the paperwork electronically."

Michelle was in the kitchen putting away the breakfast dishes and he said to his lawyer, "Hold on a moment, let me ask Michelle if that time is ok with her."

He turned to her and said, "Michelle, I have the lawyer on the line, he wants to know if Wednesday morning at ten is a good time for you to sign off on the deed for the townhouse?"

"Eric, I have been thinking about this, and I am not sure that I am doing the right thing by signing off."

Eric was stunned. He told his lawyer that he would call him back, and his hand trembled when he replaced the phone.

What was this all about, he wondered? He had not once, but several times asked her to make very sure that this was what she wanted, before they had closed the deal on the house in Hendersonville. She had been very sure, she had told him, and at that time he was convinced then that she meant it.

He looked at her, but she wouldn't meet his eyes. Now things were worse than they had been when she had wanted half the value of the townhouse. Now she had half of both. Why had he trusted her? Why hadn't they come back here first, before closing the deal on the house in North Carolina? Then she could have signed off before he plunked his money down on the other house.

He tried to get a grip on himself. He knew that unless he showed her kindness and understanding, she would just get her back up.

He was careful to explain his feelings to her and he asked her why she had now decided not to sign.

"Eric, it is not that I have definitely decided not to sign off. I am just not sure that this is the right thing for me to do right now. You know, it takes me a lot longer to think things through. That is how my mind works. I just need some more time to think about this."

"It comes down to trust, Michelle and I don't want you to feel pressured, but you were the one who wanted to come back here right away to pack, so you would be back in NC in time for the planting season."

He couldn't hold back what he wanted to say to her now and he continued, "Do you understand the unreasonableness about your demands in October, when you said that you thought you were entitled to half of the value of this townhouse, just because that is what was stated in the prenuptial? After all, we had only been married for a few months. Did you realize then, that would have been the end of our marriage? And now, after you made this latest commitment to me, how can I ever trust you again about anything? Can you at least explain to me what has put all this doubt in your mind?"

Then, she explained to him about her fears of him going back to Jane, maybe for Jamie's sake, when she had overheard him on the cell phone on the drive up. "And then, where would I be? I would have to find a job and you know Eric, in the past I have had troubles holding down any job for long. I need the security of at least having a home and some income. I didn't think the prenuptial was very fair to me in providing for my future in case our marriage would not work out."

"It did provide for you in case of my death. For all I know, you might have become tired of me after a while, or you might have wanted a younger man, who sexually could give you more of what you needed. I wasn't going to provide for your security in that way."

"Or you might have become tired of me Eric. You have been married many more times than I have and my suspicions are that there had to be some reasons for all your divorces. It couldn't all have been the faults of your ex-wives."

"I explained to you Michelle, that after my bout with cancer, I had a total shift of consciousness. I am not the same person now that I was. I don't want to have to defend myself or my actions of what went on previously in my life. That was then. I am a different person now and I ask you to trust me, based on how you see me presently. Not based on how your perceptions make you think of what might have been. In a sense I was reborn and you or anyone else cannot keep holding me responsible for however I might have behaved previously. I have already paid for that more than enough and I don't think God has put you in my life to keep holding me accountable."

"Yes but Eric, we only knew each other for such a short time before we were married and of course I would have far less doubts now if we had known each other a lot longer."

"That goes both ways Michelle, had I known about the troubles we are experiencing, I am not sure if I would have asked you to marry me. But perhaps all of this did not happen by chance. Nothing ever does, I am convinced of that. There has to be some reason for everything and perhaps we were brought together for our mutual growth. I want to believe that this latest obstacle has been put in our path for that same reason and it is up to us how we deal with it. We can either walk away from this and give up on us, or we can think of it as a process for our collective enlightenment."

She looked at him then and there was a gentleness in her eyes that he had not seen earlier. The raw fear was gone. She came over to where had had been standing, defiantly with his hands in his pant pockets and she kissed him on his cheek.

He was now terribly confused. He was unable to switch on and off like that.

"Go ahead and make that appointment with the lawyer Eric and I will sign the papers. Let's get on with our lives."

He let out a loud sigh. She had always told him that this was one of his endearing qualities, this heavy sighing, which identified him so much with his Jewishness.

He phoned the lawyer's office and confirmed the appointment.

But something in his guts told him that they hadn't quite finished with this yet.

His suspicions grew stronger on Wednesday morning

when, before Michelle went off to see her lawyer, his lawyer urged her not to take whatever this man would tell her too seriously. "He is very conscientious and he tends to take his job too serious. I made the appointment with him, because he is conveniently located in this building. Just tell him that you have decided to sign the papers and that you understand that he must talk to you about what is in your best interest. He is only doing his job."

After Eric had waited for close to an hour, he finally gave in to his concerns. He asked the paralegal to find out why this was taking so long. "Has she been kept waiting there for all this time?" he asked.

Just then his own lawyer came out of his office and he also began to wonder what went wrong. When the paralegal came back a few minutes later and said that they were still debating the issues and that they would soon be finished, Eric suspected that she had changed her mind again. He paced back and forth in the little conference room and his first impulse was that here was yet another example of how lawyers create situations which will eventually cost their clients a great deal more money. He had never fully trusted them and they had never disappointed him for feeling the way he did.

Michelle returned a little later and she immediately said to Eric, "We must talk about this some more. The lawyer advised me repeatedly not to be pressured into signing any-thing, unless I was convinced that this was in my best inter-est and I am not convinced that it is."

Eric's own lawyer joined them in their ensuing confronta-tional dialogue and said, "I spoke to him and he cannot advise her that signing would be in her best interest. I explained to him that this had been your agreement when you bought your other house in North Carolina, but he will not change his mind and he suggested that she go home and think about it some more. He would be happy to see her again after she has some more time to reflect on her decision."

Eric was fuming and begun to have difficulties in controlling his anger. Did this imbecile of a lawyer realize that he was destroying a marriage that had been very shaky almost from the beginning and only because of their collective hard work to try to save their marriage, were they together at all? Had Michelle told him about their trust issues and what the psychotherapist had told them about the townhouse in Toronto?

They went home not speaking. What was the point? Their marriage was over. She had betrayed him twice now. It was just a matter of time and he secretly wondered how nasty things would get.

He was going to have to get himself a top notch lawyer, he thought, "One which could get really nasty with Michelle in order to make her less demanding. But is this really who I am? And how could I do what I have to do and still like myself?"

Eric's lawyer phoned him the next day and explained that Michelle's lawyer had called and had suggested that if they altered the documents, he could advise her to sign them. "In the documents there is a paragraph which states that Michelle did not sign under duress," he explained. "If we strike this out Eric, then we can still register the new deed. She could of course come back to this later and claim duress in which case the deed would not hold up in court, but she would have to take this to the Ontario courts and that could be expensive. What do you think the chances are, that she would come back and take this to trial, once you both are settled in your new home in Hendersonville? This may be the best deal we can get Eric. I suggest you think about it and call me back."

Eric decided that he had nothing to lose at this point except some more legal costs for that idiot lawyer who was jerking them around.

He told Michelle that her lawyer had some other ideas he wanted to discuss with her and he made the appointment for the following morning. Then he set up an appointment with a real estate broker for that same afternoon to list his house for sale.

"Let's get this stuff all tied up so we can begin to pack and leave here," he thought. "This place has brought me nothing but a lot of grief. The sooner we can leave here, the sooner we can get on with our lives."

Live the dreams of your new reality and don't live in the past Eric, he said to himself. "You are in a process of discovering, no, a process of creating your life new each day. Don't forget the lessons of the past, but don't lock yourself into them either, for then, you will not be able to see the beauty of the here and now. Michelle is not well. What I mean is that she thinks different than most of us. Her brain functions dissimilar to mine. I need to learn to deal much better with that and for me it seems that happiness is a learning process still to be learned."

With all these good intentions, the following morning he went with Michelle to her lawyer's office and was politely asked to be seated in the waiting room, which was divided by a glass partition. Through it he could study the lawyer's facial features. Perhaps, he thought, while I am waiting, I can try to figure out what made this man so completely unconscious? Even, if he couldn't come to some conclusion about him, which was more than plausible, he would at least be able to fill the time while waiting without becoming paranoid.

The lawyer sported a small goatee, fashionable, and perfectly shaped and trimmed. He wore small but elegantly decorated turtle glasses that seem to soften his otherwise cold dark eyes which had difficulties in finding a resting place. He was a short man, probably no more than five foot four and although his dress gave the appearance of being casual, it had expensive written all over it.

Eric wouldn't have liked him, even if the man hadn't been his wife's lawyer. He probably was an elitist who thought that he was always right in his quest. A modern Don Quixote. Then he caught himself. "This is not my highest. I am being judgmental now and I am allowing my ego to get the better of me. For all I know he may be a person just like me, trying to discover who he is. We both have a purpose here on earth even though I do not like his. I too, just like this lawyer, need to grow from all of my experiences."

Finally Michelle came out well over an hour after she had entered his office. Later he learned from her that she had told him all about his arrest and the subsequent assault charge.

"No wonder," he thought. "He had not wanted her to sign off on the deed. He probably thought that he was doing her a real service by talking her out of this. As long as she was willing to keep on talking, he was willing to keep on listening. His meter was running anyways."

What was wrong with his wife for not being able to use better judgment, for not being able to conceptualize this situation better? For some time now he had known that she had a problem with this, but so what? If he loved her, he needed to learn to deal with it. Or, was she intentionally being a little coy? Was this all a ploy? Was she staging this in the same way she had done, when she had told the officer that he had been drinking when he had been arrested?

By now of course he knew well of his wife's emotional problems, but he wondered which part was triggered by her problems and which portion was triggered by just ordinary greed? Or was it caused by her insecurity? In that case, he concluded, these were probably one and the same.

What was the difference? he thought. Are not all the problems we create for ourselves and for others caused by our own mind, which causes us to fear and distrust? Part of these probably came from an evolutionary process, while the balance were fears which we added on our own, simply as a byproduct of growing up in more or less hostile environments. So, perhaps, his wife's defense mechanism kicked in more often than is the case with most of us.

If he really wanted to have a life with Michelle, he had to learn to accept what was. I can either buy into my own belief system, and allow it to become a false perception about her, he thought, or I can believe that whatever her perceptions are, she will need to deal with these herself. In time, she would need to change her mind, or her mind will eventually change her and she will become seriously disabled.

They met with the real estate agent that afternoon and Eric listed his house up for sale. The agent advised him that he should be asking more for his townhouse than he had thought to ask. "The builders have just increased the prices for the new units that are now for sale," she said, "and you have a lot of extras which you have put into your home that they are not offering."

This could well mean that he could make a small profit as opposed to the loss which he originally had expected, and he was extremely happy with his choice of agents. He was genuine, when he, on her way out, complimented her on the smart outfit she wore, but Michelle interpreted what he had said as flirtatious.

A short time after the woman left, Eric began to notice a distinct change in his wife's behavior. She became at times downright hostile and nasty. At first he wasn't too concerned. He had seen these mood swings of hers many times in the past. It seemed to him that she was perhaps angry or upset about the fact that he did not have to lose money on the sale of the townhouse as he had originally told her he might. Perhaps she thinks I purposely lied to her, to try to manipulate her into signing, he thought.

He did not want to ask her about his suspicions, nor did he want to ask her what prompted her change of attitude. What was the point? She was obviously in one of her fear moods again and he knew he was going to get some evasive answer.

He thought it was strange that his wife did not seem to want to share his happiness about the price escalation of the townhouse. How sad, he thought, that she seemed so addicted to her perceptions.

Because she had left her car in the garage of their house in Hendersonville, she had to rely on him, to take her to where ever she wanted to go. At first, he did not think that this would be too much of a problem since they wouldn't be in Toronto very long. A lot of their free time would be spend on packing up their things.

That night, after supper however, Michelle said, "Eric, I feel too cooped up here. I want you to take me to a chanting service at the Toronto Meditation Centre. Their services begin at nine and we will need to hurry as it is quite far from here to Dupont Street."

Eric didn't really feel much like going out that night. He preferred that they would start to pack their things. Besides, he couldn't see much sense in driving all that way, just to be involved in some sort of a chanting service. He knew better than to argue with her though, when she was in one of her moods, and he accepted what was.

She was however rushing him consistently and seemed not to want to miss any opportunity to pick a fight.

"Eric, are you driving slowly on purpose just so that we will be late?" Or, "I know where it is and you are going the wrong way. Are you doing this intentionally?"

But of course he knew perfectly well how to get there.

"I knew it was a mistake to leave my car in Hendersonville. Now I have to depend on you and your stupid ways of driving to take me everywhere."

It took him almost superhuman control not to get into an argument with her. It was very clear to him that she wanted to initiate a fight.

It would have been almost too easy for him to tell her how wrong she was in what she was doing, but he knew that would have been his ego gaining control over the situation, and there was no way he was going to allow this to happen. Again, he was pleased that he was able to look at himself in that way. It was almost like there was another voice telling him not to go there.

He realized just how far he had come and he was grateful for whatever had brought them together, causing him to stretch and to grow to this point.

But when they came home later that night, she still seemed very angry with him and she said, "Eric, I don't like the way you have treated me tonight. I think I will sleep in the other bedroom."

This was getting to be her way of punishing him he thought. For what, he could not imagine.

"If by doing this, it makes you feel better about yourself, then I think you should sleep in the spare bedroom." He went over to where she was standing, but all he saw in her eyes was intense fear. Yet, all he had wanted to do was to give her a goodnight kiss.

Instead, he decided to just wish her a goodnight and he walked back to their bedroom. She did not respond and he gently closed the door as he went to bed.

He was exhausted, but sleep did not come easy. In his heart, he knew that there was a higher purpose to all this, but in his mind he kept asking himself why he was letting her get away with this kind of disrespectful behavior. Perhaps he should become more aggressive, he thought, then maybe she might respect him more. But he knew intuitively, that this was not the answer he had been searching for. For some weird reason his thoughts went to his father then.

Jakob had been from the old school, and if Eric's mother had ever dared to behave that way, his dad would have severely punished her for it. Eric knew of course that this kind of aggressiveness would not solve their problems. On the contrary, Jakob had been feared much more than loved by his family.

The next morning, Michelle seemed to have all but forgotten about her nastiness. She was eager to get started packing and Eric was elated by the change in her. They went out to buy the necessary packing supplies but they had only just got started packing, when she asked him if she could use his car.

"I want to go up to the Waldorf centre, there is supposed to be a meeting for abused women there and I would like to go."

"It is only a short distance from here, Michelle, I don't mind driving you there. I don't know when you would return and in the meantime, I might need the car for something or other. I can continue to pack things here and when you are ready to be picked up, just give me a call."

He had previously experienced her going off without calling him to say that she was going to be late. She might not return until many hours later. He would then be worried about her.

She never did like being turned down by him. He knew that she had problems in dealing with rejection and perhaps he was a bit controlling about this, or maybe he was just overreacting, but he didn't like being without his car in case he needed it. What was the difference, he thought, as long as she got to go where she wanted to.

She phoned him much later that afternoon. "Eric, the meeting was very good for me, it helped me to see things more clearly. Afterwards, I went to their library and sat and read some of their books for a while, that's why I am a bit late. You know, I have always been interested in the Waldorf system. Eric, can you please pick me up? I shall be waiting for you outside the library."

Shortly after they returned and when he had just started to make their supper, a friend of hers phoned.

After she had hung up the phone, she said, "There is a special worship service this evening at the Airport Church, Eric. They will have some very special guest speakers tonight. I read a lot about them years ago when I was with the Born Again Christian movement in Clearwater. I would very much like to go."

"What time does it start? You came home pretty late and we still haven't had supper yet."

The part about coming home pretty late, he decided, he could have left out, but it came out before he had a chance to think about it.

"He said we should be there by eight."

"Michelle, it is now almost six. I still have to make supper. It will take us at least an hour to drive out there. I think that this is rushing things a bit too much. I am pretty tired, I have been packing up and boxing our things all day long. Could we please skip it?"

"Eric, every time I ask you to take me somewhere, you make me feel like a criminal. I need to get out once in a while. You just want to keep me cooped up here all the time. That is being abusive."

He didn't want to have a scene again so he simply made a hash out of the meatloaf he had been planning to cook. They ate their supper in silence and he phoned her friend back to ask for directions.

She wanted to drive, because she said she knew exactly where it was. "This will save time," she said.

Perhaps he should have let her drive, but he was concerned because this was Friday night, it was raining hard and it was at the height of rush hour traffic. He knew that she didn't yet know her way through the city as well as he did.

She argued of course, but when he asked her to explain precisely how to get there, the way she explained it was not at all how her friend had directed him. When he told her, she began to antagonize him again.

She commented on how dangerous he was driving. "You are going to get us both killed, because you are too damn stubborn to let me drive."

She repeatedly told him to pull over to let her drive. "Eric, you don't see as well driving at night. Why don't you admit it?"

Finally he told her, "Shut up Michelle. If you can't keep your mouth shut, I am going to ask you to get out of my car. You are a menace to us both."

"Sure, you have me at your mercy now, that's what you always wanted. If I had my own car, I would have gone by myself. I wouldn't have needed you."

Then, she was quiet for a while and he thought that she

had finally given up. But the quiet didn't last long. Now she begun to recite her Hail Mary's over and over again and when he asked her to stop, she answered, "The way you are driving, I think I need Her protection. You are always trying to stop me from practicing my religious convictions. I should tell the authorities about this, perhaps they should lock you up again."

He shivered. Not because it was cold in the car, but because he could not understand why she was this evil. It frightened him and he was glad when they finally came to the street where the church was located.

He thought of telling her that she had been dead wrong in the way she had given him the driving directions, but he thought, "What was the use of that?" She was in one of her moods again and it was best to let it go at that. He didn't need to win, but he did want her to treat him with the same dignity that he treated her. Just because she was ill, he did not have to accept her abuse.

When she was like that, she really needed help, perhaps some medication that would balance her. He had discussed this with her some time ago, but she wouldn't hear of it. "There is nothing wrong with me Eric," she had said. "I am not about to put harmful chemicals into my body just because you think so."

She had asked him to drop her off in front of the church. It was still raining hard. He couldn't drop her right in front, there were simply too many people, it was impossible to pull up. He had never seen a church that was so well attended.

He dropped her as close as he could, but she still had to walk a bit in the rain.

Before, while they had been driving and when she had said her untold many Hail Mary's, she had been holding her rosary beads and he noticed when he dropped her off, that she was still holding them.

He found a parking space about a mile from the church. There were so many people, trying to find a space anywhere they could, that Eric considered himself fortunate to have found something not too terrible far away.

He became drenched of course and he thought to himself, What we don't do for love. He grinned as he walked through the streaming downpour.

He found Michelle, a short distance from the entrance, looking down as though she had lost something.

"What have you lost, Michelle?" he asked.

He was surprised when she responded. "I have lost the Virgin Mary and a number of beads. She must have fallen off my rosary. I have looked everywhere, and I am soaked, but I can not find Her."

"I am sorry honey, we can buy another one. Let's go in now, it is really wet out here."

"Buying another one, is not the same thing Eric. This one was given to me by a very special friend."

As they entered the church, he couldn't help but wonder if there hadn't been some sort of a message in this for her. He hoped that she would think of it that way as well, but she would never tell him of course.

Pity he thought. We would learn the lessons we need to learn a lot faster, if we would defy our egos and expose our vulnerability some times. All we seem to be doing, is to keep the universe waiting longer and longer for the human race to finally wake up.

The building was massive, and there were people all around praying and yelling to God and Jesus Christ. There was something taking place on the podium, but he couldn't clearly see what it was, nor could he hear because of the distraction all around him. Some people were laying on the floor and beating their heads on the carpet.

He sat there for several hours, in some sort of a trance about what was going on there.

Why did these people have to work so hard just to find God? he wondered. Can't they understand that they have already found Him in themselves?

Finally she got up and she seemed ready to leave.

"You know Eric," she said, "a few years ago I went to this same kind of Christian church in Clearwater. I searched for God a long time there, but then, when I couldn't find Him, I lost interest in the way they worshipped. This was at a time in my life when I was very confused. But I am glad we came here tonight, just so you could experience this as well."

On the way back to his car, they looked for her Virgin Mary. She found it, but a car had run over her little idol and she cried for most of the drive back.

He didn't know if she cried for the loss of the Virgin or for the way she had acted on their way there. Perhaps both were in some way connected, he thought

By the time they came home, she had stopped crying. Again she told him that she was going to sleep in the other bedroom.

"When you learn to treat me better, Eric, we will sleep together again. As for now, I feel safer being in my own space."

This time, all he could do was to shrug his shoulders. He was keenly aware that he didn't bother to wish her good-night.

He remained awake thinking of how horribly ill she was. He had begun to feel very unsafe himself now. She might just decide to phone the cops again and have him arrested a second time.

The thought briefly crossed his mind that it might be better to just pack up all of her things and to drive her to North Carolina as soon as possible. It could be safer he thought, to leave her there and for him to return to the townhouse here in Toronto.

He didn't want to make a decision about that at this moment. He would have to talk to her about this first and he had to be very careful about the timing because of her mood swings.

He himself needed more time to think this through. "I can't make a rational decision feeling the way I do now. I am much to tired. Best to get some sleep and think about this some more tomorrow."

Chapter
SEVENTEEN

The next day, Eric woke very early and he decided to quietly go downstairs to continue to pack. He planned to box Michelle's things separately, just in case her things would need to be shipped to Hendersonville without including his.

We have such a strange way of thinking, he decided, or maybe it was just his way of thinking. In his mind, he was already dividing his things from hers, yet he had not yet made any decision as to what he planned to do. They were still married of course, but now their things had already become his or hers. Deliberate thoughts were dangerous because, more often than not, we make them become reality. In a way, we convince ourselves, and the more we become convinced, the more real it becomes. He concluded that our thoughts are not always our most loving or useful human traits, helpful as these might be at times when we need to reach our goals.

Michelle came down at about nine. Since he was busy packing and boxing things using the kitchen table, she made herself some breakfast and ate silently in their dining room. She didn't offer to help him but instead she read for a while out of the many books she used for self improvement.

Sometimes she reads too much of this stuff, he decided. She gets herself confused because she is trying so hard to become a better person and she takes everything that was ever written about this as her gospel. A good way to become a better person, he thought somewhat cynically, would simply be by offering to help me pack.

But he didn't want to say that to her, because he knew that she would resent it or be hurt by it and he wanted to avoid getting her upset all over again.

After a while, she went upstairs to make a phone call and he wondered why she did not make the call from the downstairs phone, but when she came back down, he understood what had been the reasons for her need for privacy.

"Eric, I just made an appointment to see the nurse who treated me after you assaulted me last October. Can you please drive me there? It is not very far."

He was shocked. She had never told him that she had gone to see a nurse. Why would she have done that, he had not hurt her! There had to be some other reason, he concluded.

"Yes, Michelle. Do you know about how long you will be? Jane asked me to pick Jamie up from school and bring her to her skating practice."

"It should take a little over an hour. You could drop me off and then do your thing for Jamie."

"Ok, when you are done with your appointment, call me. I will keep my cell on." He normally didn't like to keep his cell phone on. Callers could leave messages either on his cell or at home. He disliked getting interrupted by cell phones and he pitied those who had become enslaved to them.

"Can you tell me why you want to see this nurse now, almost six months after you claim that I assaulted you?"

He wanted to say to her that he had not done any of the things she had accused him of, but what was the point? She was completely convinced about the incident. There was no way he could possibly change her mind.

"I just want to talk to her about the things you and I talked about a while ago Eric. You remember, on the drive back here from Hendersonville? You said that if we could prove to each other that it did not happen the way I say it did, perhaps by taking a lie detector test, then that could dispel a lot of these trust issues we have between us."

He didn't immediately respond to her. If she was serious about that, it could indeed change a great deal of things between them.

He dropped her off in front of the hospital and just as he arrived at the skating arena to drop Jamie off, she called him on the cell to let him know that she was done.

Strange, he thought, that she did not say anything about how her appointment went. But then he realized that she probably thought that Jamie was still in his car and at any rate, that was not the way she did things.

He drove back across town and she was waiting for him outside the hospital. He looked at her as she walked up to the car. She was so damn cute. He let out one of his deep sighs. It would be hard if not impossible for anyone who didn't know her well, to believe that she had such a horrible emotional problem.

As she got into his car, he would have liked to immediately begin questioning her about her appointment, but he knew that she would resent this and he contained his eagerness and decided to wait for her to volunteer what he wanted to know.

When they came home however, he couldn't contain himself any longer and said, "Michelle, you will probably tell me about how your appointment went in your own good time, but the outcome of what this nurse told you is very important to us and our relationship. I am dying to find out how it went."

"The nurse said that you had no rights in forcing me to take a lie detector test. She said that this was so obviously abusive behavior and that if you continue to ask me to do this, I should call the police and make a formal complaint."

Eric was totally stunned. What in heaven's name had she told that nurse? Now he could also better understand how her conversation with her attorney had gone and why he had been so dead set against her signing anything.

"If she had come to me," he thought, "with that cute and innocent look of hers and the way she was able to articulate these distortions, I would of course believe her completely. I would feel that I would want to do anything I could to protect her from that evil and aggressive husband of hers."

Now, he finally begun to see how dangerous his position really was and he decided to talk to her after supper about driving her to Hendersonville as soon as possible. He would make sure that she had her hot bath first. He knew that she was always a little better then, and more relaxed.

That night, turned out not to be a good night for her. He sensed her fear and anxieties, and he decided to wait for a better opportunity.

Two days later, after he had almost completely packed all her things, he saw an opportunity. She seemed in high spirits that morning and he did not see the usual fear that he normally could detect in her eyes. Instead, they were clear and brilliant.

By now, he knew what signs to look for. Her eyes would be green in color and expressed such a deep sadness, agony and sorrow, that it would break his heart to see her that way. He knew then that the fears she felt were very real for her. But this morning they looked out on her world, clear and unafraid.

"Michelle, I have been thinking. We have been arguing a lot lately. You are without your car and I think I can understand how that must make you feel. I have almost finished packing up all of your things. I can pack mine later when I return. Why don't I drive you up this Sunday? This way you can unpack your things leisurely and I won't have to feel pressured because of you being without your car. Besides, I think we can use a little rest from each other. What do you think?"

"I think that would be great Eric. I am really excited about getting to our new home to begin getting things organized. Sunday sounds good to me. Will the weather be ok for driving?"

"The long range forecast promises a good driving day on Sunday. In Canada, you never know in March about the weather, so let's plan on doing that."

He felt bad not telling her the truth about his own fears. About not being able to tell her that he no longer felt safe with her, because of her constant mood changes. He felt that he was deceiving her a little, but he knew of no other way to make her feel comfortable about going sooner.

"Actually Michelle, we are only going a few weeks earlier than we had originally planned to go. This will give me time to pack up the balance, and make arrangements for our furniture to be shipped."

Somehow he felt a little better about adding that, perhaps not so much for her sake as for his own.

Besides, he needed more time by himself, to think all this through. He really had not decided anything, but he thought it would be good for them to be apart for a while, just so he could sort all of this out more clearly.

He thought about her illness and he didn't think it was right for him to leave her, just because she was ill. Again he thought that if the shoe was on the other foot, he could well imagine how he would feel.

Sure, she had refused up to this point to seek medical help to get medication for her condition, but perhaps when she was on her own, out there, by herself, she might be able think about this in a more positive way.

They left very early Sunday morning. Both of them were up well before daylight and Michelle seemed bright and cheerful that morning.

They had their breakfast while driving. Michelle had prepared sandwiches, just so they could drive straight through without having to make frequent stops. She was excited and happily chattering away about what plans she had, once they were settled.

They even sang some songs together. This was something they had done occasionally during their happier days, during the romantic phase in their early relationship.

Eric hummed along with her, but deep inside, he felt very sad. Why couldn't life be this way always?

He didn't have answers except spiritually he knew that nothing happened quite by accident. They were brought together for a reason, he had to believe that.

The way she was now, why did he have to rush her off? Why couldn't it have waited until they were ready to leave together? He started to feel that he might have been much too impatient with her and that perhaps it had been a mistake to leave so soon. He began to doubt his own reasons—that major flaw in his character—he had always been much too eager to make hasty decisions.

He had learned, while he was recovering from cancer, about compassion and understanding. Shouldn't that also apply to his wife?

The trip was a delight for the most part, until they were several hundred miles from Hendersonville.

He could almost see the transformation taking possession of her, like the shadows of a cloud on a summer's day, spreading over the smooth surface of a small lake on an otherwise cloudless afternoon.

She asked him to take the Blue Mountain Parkway because it would be such a beautiful drive through the mountains.

Eric was caught off guard by her request, only because things had been so very pleasant up to that point and he was concerned about what might happen if he refused her. By now it was close to twilight and besides, it was raining and a little foggy. She would not be able to see what ordinarily would have been a very beautiful and scenic drive.

He expressed his concerns to her. "It is only a two lane road Michelle, full of many dangerous S-turns and the speed limit is forty miles per hour. It will add many hours to our trip." And then it came.

"Here you go again spoiling everything Eric by being so controlling. If you are concerned about driving the Parkway, why don't you let me drive for a while? You have been driving most of the day without asking me to take a turn. What are you afraid of?"

He wouldn't give in to her, and she demanded that he turn around and go back about a dozen or so miles to the entrance of the Parkway.

Eric did what she wanted, much against his better judgment. He would try to keep things on a positive note for as long as this was possible.

For a short distance, after she had taken over the driving, all went well. She seemed happy again and said, "Eric, you worry too much. It takes all the fun out of being with you. You see, it is quite all right and the views are truly magnificent, even if it is cloudy and a little foggy. Don't you believe in adventures any longer?"

He was almost convinced that he had done the right thing by conceding to take the Parkway after all. "You see," he thought, "all it takes to deal with her mood swings is to have a little more acceptance."

Then, almost all of a sudden, darkness set in and she was forced to slow down to about twenty miles per hour. Even at that speed they had trouble seeing more than a few dozen feet ahead of them, mostly because of the rapidly thickening fog. Sometimes she had to break very hard to prevent from hitting a deer.

He began to feel very unsafe with her apparent lack of driving skills on these treacherous roads and for her inability to concede that it was high time to find a solution to their dilemma.

He thought, if we hit anything at all out here in the boonies, we will be unable to find help and my cell does not work up here in the mountains. I have not seen another car for the last hour and no one will know that we are having troubles.

It was also getting colder now, and he began to see that the rain was occasionally changing to wet snow up in these higher altitudes. Great, he thought, that's all we need, a blinding snowstorm.

He finally demanded that she pull off the road so he could turn on the cabin light in order to see on his map where the next turn-off would be.

At first she refused flatly, but finally, after he had patiently explained the dangers of perhaps having to spend the night out here, she also seemed to become more frightened and turned onto a soft shoulder. She got out of the car and told him violently that he could drive himself all the way home.

"You are a very domineering personality and you really should see a doctor. This is not healthy. I don't want to live with you when you behave like that. You have a dangerous streak in you, and it is no wonder that the police arrested you for assault. They must have seen how dangerous you can be."

Eric quietly continued to study the map and he spotted a turn-off. He didn't know how far they had driven, but he guessed it couldn't be too far. They couldn't have done much better than thirty miles since they pulled off the interstate. He could not be absolutely sure if they had already passed the turn-off that he had spotted on the map. He had seen some signs before, but because of the heavy fog and the intense darkness, he had been unable to read them.

It seemed to him that they had been driving for hours, but when he looked at his watch, it had only been less than an hour.

Finally, he spotted the turn-off. He let out an audible sigh of relief. Had they missed the turn-off, there would not have been another one for at least several hours, and he wouldn't have liked driving under these conditions any longer than he absolutely had to.

It was ten by the time they were able to rejoin the interstate again. He was exhausted, and he was sure that she was equally drained. It would be at least another three hours until they would be home and he decided to stop at a restaurant to get a cup of coffee and something to eat.

Intuitively, he knew not to talk to her about what had happened during the past few hours. Firstly they were both very tired, which was certainly not a good time to try to talk to her about her inability to take rejection, and secondly, what good would it do?

Michelle was in one of her extremely nasty moods again and Eric knew now for certain that he must not remain in their home in Hendersonville any longer than was absolutely necessary.

He wished that he could unload all of her things out of his car as soon as they arrived, then he could start driving back immediately, but he was far too exhausted to do that.

When they arrived home, she again said, "Eric, I will sleep in the spare bedroom. I don't feel safe sleeping in the same room with you," but he was used to her rejections by now. Funny, he thought, the more you get rejected, the better you learn to deal with them.

He emptied out the SUV with the last vestige of strength and collapsed into a restless sleep.

The next morning, he woke bolt upright. He thought he had heard a noise just outside the windows. It was still too dark outside and he could barely distinguish the abundance of the heavy spring foliage in front the bedroom windows.

He looked at his watch and he saw that it was just six o'clock.

He recalled the night before and speculated as to what she was doing up so early and how she would be this morning.

He quickly showered and came into the kitchen to make coffee. He hoped she would be better. He did not want to leave her here all by herself with her being so very angry.

She came into the kitchen and when he said, "Good morning Michelle," she did not respond. He looked at her then, a bit more closely. It didn't look like she had slept much, he decided. Usually, she prided herself on her appearance, but this morning she had put no make-up on. Her face was pasty white, much paler even than her normal natural complexion, for she had beautiful fair skin. Her eyes again expressed intense agony and fear.

He asked her if she wanted some coffee but she declined. "I am not going to drink any more coffee Eric, I don't think it agrees with me. After we had the cup of coffee late last night, I couldn't sleep very well and my tummy has been upset ever since."

He still had not actually decided to leave immediately. He did not want to leave her in the lurch like this and thought that if he stayed a few days, just to help her get settled, this might be better. Besides, he was still pretty tired from the long drive yesterday and he thought a few days of rest would do him good.

They had their meager breakfast. There were only a few things left in the fridge. They had been too late arriving and could not shop for groceries at that late hour.

"Eric," she said, "I have thought about things a lot during the night and I do not think it is safe for us to be together. You are a very angry person and I am concerned for what you might do to me out here in the boonies. This morning I am going to see about getting some sort of support from the authorities here. I am really scared about being out here all alone with you."

He had to keep reminding himself that she was ill. Or, did she have other motives? It is so hard to tell, he thought. But then he thought, it is all the same, these motives are there because she is ill.

"There is no need for you to be in fear any longer, Michelle. I am going to leave here as soon as I can pack up some of my things. I want to try to get back to Toronto late tonight. I think you should try to get some help while I am in Toronto. You really need to be able to try to see things differently than the way you do now. As long as you continue to think of me as your enemy, as the bad guy, I will continue to be as you see me. I am not your enemy. The enemy is inside of your head. It is your perceptions about me, caused by your previous relationships, your pains and hurts. If only you could begin to see me in the way I really am, but I don't think that will happen until you get the help you need."

Before he left for the long drive back and with a heavy heart and much sadness, he walked over to where she was standing to try to give her a hug, but she backed away from him. Intense fear was written all over her eyes and face.

Chapter
EIGHTEEN

He backed out of their driveway slowly, hoping that she would call him back. But she didn't.

Deep in thought he drove the short distance to the entrance of the interstate and he almost took it going southbound instead of north.

There wasn't any point in pondering the imponderable. Had it just been bad luck, that he had been so much attracted to her a little over a year ago? He doubted it. He knew that his experiences over the past few years, had taught him a lot about himself and he was sure he had grown a great deal in learning how to love without putting the many conditions onto the relationship that he had been guilty of previously.

Guilty, he thought, is really not the right word here. Regrets maybe. Guilt is when you know you have done something that wasn't your highest or your best. He simply hadn't known what it was he had been doing, that had been so terribly wrong. But then, so hadn't a lot of men from his generation.

"In those days, we didn't think about relationships in quite the same way. We were simply too busy trying to become successful. We didn't realize then, that success wasn't measured on how much money you made or what latest model sports car you could afford.

"Wasn't that the whole point of learning and growing? Isn't that how we as humans evolve? Isn't all of what we learn with which we created our adaptive qualities part of the evolutionary process of our species?"

Perhaps the reason why he had been married so many times was that none of his previous partners had been aware of his gradual transition and thus, this collective growth ingredient had been missing in those relationships.

Being married to Michelle, he didn't know if their growth had been reciprocal. She had never shared this with him. But then, she only would have benefited from their relationship to the point of her own understanding, of her own truth.

He remembered, when he had first discovered that he had cancer, how he had been so angry with God. Why me? he had cried out in agony.

Now, he had to admit, that he had become a far better person since those days. Now, he was not angry, not at all. Not with her, not with God and not even with himself for having failed again in this latest relationship. Frustrated perhaps, because she didn't seem to be able to comprehend, that when a spouse attempts to take monetary advantage of her partner, that partnership comes to an end because the trust is forever gone between them.

Back then, he would have asked how he could have allowed himself to make such a horrible mistake. Now, he understood that any resentment he might have, would create a negative energy which would contaminate his entire being.

Watch the thoughts your mind is creating, he thought. Be present and mindful, observe them for what they are.

Don't allow your ego to create an environment of anger and hate. You have a choice, Eric. Don't feel that you have been taken advantage of. Just be in the present moment and let go of the past.

It was even now possible for him to conclude that her illness, her insecurity and her apparent greed, which made her act the way she had, were intrinsically related and came from the same fear based origin.

He let his mind wander freely now as he drove on and he had the strangest sensation of being able to observe his own thoughts. This is almost like having another self, he thought, a self which had remained unaffected by all the negatives which had been part of his life, a self which was completely uncontaminated. How sweet is that? He asked his other self.

Thoughts, he rationalized, are only the results of calling into being his past experiences, or they were the consequences of his planning and worrying about what would happen in the future.

In the past, he had allowed his thought process far too often to become part of his actions or reactions. This would create false perceptions and fears. The past is not who you are right now, and the future hasn't yet happened, he decided.

By learning to become more conscious, we are speeding up our own evolution and by doing so, we also help to evolve all others and all else. What we do, who we are and how we interact with others, has to make a difference in this world, he thought.

He had just bypassed Asheville and he decided to take a quick coffee break and to have something to eat as well. He hadn't had much of a breakfast, he realized and at any rate, he needed to stop for gas.

As he pulled up at a Denny's, he was reminded that he and Michelle had stopped there once. That thought made him sad. If he drove back now, and if he took her in his arms, he wondered, would she be any different? Would she be happy that he came back, or was she happy just to have the house to herself? Thoughts again, he concluded, don't give them control over your life Eric.

A short time later, he was back on the interstate again, feeling better now that he had eaten something. After a while, he began to ponder about what he should do. Should he proceed with selling his home in Toronto? Perhaps it would be better, he decided, to wait and see. Maybe she would get the help she needed. If not and in the event that he did sell his house, he would have no place to live as long as she continued to create these dreadful fears in her mind. That was not a way to live in peace!

He wondered how and when she had become so terribly disturbed. Certainly before they had been married, there had never been any indication that she had a serious emotional problem.

Perhaps her two selves interact in some weird way, he thought. Normally, as is the case with most people, some balance is achieved. In Michelle's situation it seemed to create some inner conflict and resulted in disharmony. Her outer self, affected by so many of her past experiences, and her inner self, her sweet innocence, that portion of her, to which he had been so very much attracted. That seemed like a reasonable explanation, he thought, although he was sure that most psychiatrists would probably disagree with him.

Interesting, he thought, the more that our species becomes our outer self; the results of our often distorted perceptions, the more we seem to rush toward the chaos that we ourselves create.

How can we ever create a new world order, that could function without those perceptions, which have caused such bad judgment in our thinking, making us decide that some of us are better than others?

Because of our religious teachings, we conclude that Jews are the Chosen People. This very teaching, he mused, has caused us to become terribly judgmental and to a large extent, could have been responsible for our own religious persecutions.

Nothing blinds us more than a fixed mental image, nothing kills our love for one another quicker than our own fears.

He noticed a sign which said, "Statesville and Interstate 77." Good, he thought, I have already gone a little better than one hundred miles. Only another twelve hours or so to go, until I get home. He did not feel as tired as he thought he would be and he was hopeful that he would be able to drive the balance all the way through, without having to stop for the night.

All of this contemplation makes it easier for me to drive. In a sense, it is like a diversion, he thought. It keeps my mind more active, and who knows, by the time I get home, I may have it all figured out, and perhaps, I might even be able to solve some of the problems which face our world. He grinned to himself. Thank God I have my sense of humor left, he thought. Life could be terribly boring without it.

As he entered the ramp to the interstate, his thoughts again took on a different direction. Would it really ever be possible for Michelle and I to overcome the traumatic experience we both went through last October? he thought. There were so many things which had remained unspoken.

Did she earnestly believe that he had tried to choke her? Was this an illusion of hers, a leftover from some pains she had suffered when she was a child, or had it been a ploy to terminate a marriage she had never wanted in the first place? Or alternatively, by rationalizing the choking incident in her mind, it would be a lot easier for her to validate her actions to get rewarded for her perceived injuries and thus demanding monetary compensation by insisting that she was entitled to one half of his house because of her suffering.

He realized now, perhaps better than ever before, that in order for them to remain together in a loving relationship, they had to regain the lost trust between them and the most important ingredient for trust was truth. But how would he ever know which was truth or, for that matter, how could she?

Firstly, she would need to also realize and understand above all, that there was no reason whatsoever for them to remain together in any relationship, unless there was genuine love between them.

But how could he tell her all this? She was always so ready to become defensive or, she would change the subject altogether and they would never find their way back to these important issues. They usually would get all tangled up with something else she wanted to talk about. Did she do this in order to escape self-examination? he wondered.

If indeed, her mind had played a trick on her and had created this illusion of the so-called assault, than he could possibly come to terms with that, providing she would get the help she needed. Without her getting medication to stabilize her thought process, he would be taking a chance on being arrested again and again.

But could he leave her and terminate their marriage for having this emotional problem? He had two previously failed marriages to warn him not to give up on this one so easily. This marriage, where he had finally discovered this incredible love he had felt for her.

No, he thought, but the real question was, how could he get her to commit to seeking medical help for her problems? It would be best, for the time being, for him to remain in Toronto until she had made that decision. And even then, he would have to be very careful that she would go through with the medication. She had made commitments before and not kept them.

It could also be quite possible that his own mind was not as objective as he would like to believe and that his own perceptions got in the way of him clearly seeing reality.

She could well refuse to get the help she needed if she thought there wasn't anything wrong with her and that this was all of his doing. He had heard horror stories of how mentally ill people ruined their lives and the lives of their loved ones by never admitting to themselves that they had a problem.

If she refused to get help, then the dangers for him would remain the same, and the obvious answer of course, he thought, was that he should not have to put his life and safety in jeopardy at his age.

Then, a horrible thought occurred to him. "Suppose it really did happen the way she claimed it had. Suppose, as Sandy had mentioned, he had been temporarily out of his mind, possibly because of his own early childhood experiences." In that case, he was doing her a grave injustice and he was throwing away this God given opportunity for any true happiness.

He knew that he loved her, but did she love him enough? Was their love for one another sufficiently strong to be able to withstand the pain of discovering the truth about what had really happened? Would either of them be able to cope with that?

He thought about that intently for a few minutes and concluded that he knew himself well enough to know that he was incapable of assaulting anyone, least of all his wife, the person he loved. But what if he was wrong? There was always that remote possibility. Consciously, he could never do anything like that, but what if something in his subconscious mind had somehow triggered this unthinkable behavior?

Even if he offered her the money that she believed she was entitled to, and if she accepted it, that wouldn't really prove anything and it still would be the end of their marriage. He would always still have this gnawing question, which would remain unanswered forever.

But how important was it for him to discover the answers? What did it matter, who did what? As long as they both were able to accept a portion of the responsibilities, and not ever try to go back into the past, could they then in time rediscover the trust, which had been lost that night in October?

He decided that all of this dialogue with himself was not going to help him see things any more clearly.

There were similarities here with some of the past experiences of his life, he thought. Just like now, there had always been several paths open for him to take, and each time he had hoped that he would take the one path which would eventually lead to his greater understanding and knowledge.

It reminded him of the story of a poor unfortunate beggar, who also had a choice to make, when at dusk, he was confronted on his path by a big rock, which unbeknownst to him turned out to be a sack of gold. Had he kicked against it, he would have ruined his already torn sandals, thus he carefully stepped over the rock, saving his dilapidated sandals without ever discovering the hidden treasures: the knowledge and the understanding, which he would have gained from that experience, and . . . of course the sack of gold, both lost forever.

Life is like that, he concluded. He would have to make a decision. He sure was not going to "get it" by doing nothing . . . by stepping over it.

Then, like a bolt of lighting, a thought occurred to him. Like a luminous and brilliant white cloud. The thought was so simple and beautiful, he was sure, that it was a manifestation of his God-self: They would need to eventually talk in a peaceful manner, without those constant interruptions and this side-tracking away from the subject of their discussions. But how to do this in her somewhat troubled state of mind?

She loved reading. He would write this book for her!

But first, he would have to ask her a very crucial question: if love to her meant that she would give it freely *only* if he would give in to her demands? If so, he would then in some way and very carefully have to convey to her that this was not love, but that this was called "trading."

Did she understand, as he did, that neediness and expectations where one of the most destructive things in any loving relationship?

"Don't love me for what you can get from me, love me for who I am and for who I will need to become and you Michelle must play a major part in my becoming, just as I will need to play a part in your becoming." Had he told her this, when she had said that she wanted to marry him?

"It is one thing to understand the significance of this statement, it is quite another to believe in it so strongly, that living it becomes a testimonial of that very wisdom," he had said.

If she really did believe in those principals now, at this very moment, after she had read this book, then nothing else mattered. Whatever she had wanted from him in October was no longer an issue. Michelle would have grown and learned from her own experiences, just as he had, to such an extent, that their trust in each other would be restored. They would then truly be living in the present without fear or distrust.

Under those circumstances, he and she could both forget the past and they could put the issue to rest. He would not have to live in terror again, that her fear and her insecurity would make her act in the way that had caused him so much pain that night in October.

In the past, he had always sought to experience who he was through others, rather than allowing others to experience who they were through him.

All his life, he had altered who he was, in order to change what others were thinking about him. Thus, he had lived most of his life how he wanted to be seen, not who he really was. He knew, he needed to change that part of himself, irregardless of what might happen between them.

He needed to learn to find his own center, his own inner truth, his own authenticity. He, irregardless of what Michelle's response would be, would need to learn to throw away all the protective wrappers of his own past.

What was the point of living at all, he thought, if one has to spend a major part of one's life hiding behind these acquired protections? Who and what was he protecting from, except from his own self and his own ego?

Never stop exploring who you are, he thought, for it brings you to the next level.

Our gifts become so much of nothing,
If we have been given the inspiration to write,
And yet we have not ever written,
The music we have been gifted to hear,
And we have not sung out,
Observing the beauty of nature all around us,
And we have not yet drawn it to memory,
If we have been gifted the gift of love,
And we have never truly love,
Or the gift of greatness,
And have never expressed it so,
For once you have expressed it,
You will know that you are,
Recreate yourself anew in every moment of the now,
Express yourself in that greatness and you will finally know,
WHO YOU ARE.

We are all one. One wisdom, one consciousness. We co-create, with our universe and with our God-self and we control our growth, our destiny and who we collectively become. We are all part of the same, one force, that one consciousness, thus, what we do to others, we do also to ourselves.

My dearest Michelle,
If have I hurt you, I have hurt me as well,
If I have loved you, I have loved also me,
If I have lied to you, I have lied to myself,
When I embraced you, I embraced me.
And, when I respect you, I respect myself.

EPILOGUE

For a brief moment he allowed himself to think back to his more youthful days. Those days, when he had been so very restless—when he had thought that the wife he'd married was a woman he could love because she was perfect for him. Perfect not only physically and in the way she looked, but who also had the gift to emotionally and intellectually stimulate him—and when this didn't happen, when he thought enough time had passed, he would become restless and he would think of how unlucky he had been for not having found a wife who could love him for who *he* was. Then, he would be off to find the next romance, the next marriage and the next one after that.

Now, thinking about Michelle, after not having seen her for almost two years and not having spoken to her for a good six months, he realized perhaps for the fist time in his life, how wrong he had been about his previous relationships. He now began to earnestly question if he himself had not been the cause for these failed marriages? He had not ever tried to understand the women he had been married to. He had not allowed himself to become close enough and to more intimately know and fully understand their personalities. *He had failed to love them for who they were*—always looking for and, of course, inevitably finding their shortcomings. It had really never been about that he had been unable to find someone who could love him for who *he* was—instead, it had always been about that *he* had never understood the language of love at all, he had never been able to understand the basic principal that loving someone was about understanding and indeed celebrating those difference between them. Those differences, which he had always looked upon as *their* defectiveness; *their* flaws or failures.

Not this time. This time the God of his understanding had obviously given him one final shot at it—one last time to show him once and for all that which he should have learned eons ago—before it would be too late. That God had put in his path this woman, who had been deeply troubled, a woman who was quite flawed, and to love her would be an everyday test of how well he had learned these lessons of life.

In his daily meditation, he would often concentrate on the true meaning of the word "*understanding.*" He would think of this and sometimes it would help him to separate it in two separate words, *under* and *standing* and this would make it clear to him that he really had to stand apart from himself in order to see others. He rationalized then, that from understanding came acceptance and empathy and then it became so much easier to be tolerant and compassionate, from which love could flow more abundantly.

He had loved Michelle, he decided, but again for the wrong reasons as he had failed to see that she had been wired so totally different from the way he was. Why had it been so difficult for him to accept their differences? Why hadn't he understood then that many of her actions had been out of fear. Her fear, that if he were to ever find out about her many idiosyncrasies, he would dump her, as he had done so often in the past to others. A past that she knew all too well. Fear alone can make people behave in despicable ways, he decided. All one had to do was to look at the horrific behavior of ethnic cleansing that is going on in the world, still to this day. He assumed that this was also about not accepting the diversities of human differences.

He was, of course, enormously surprised when she phoned him one day, completely out of the blue and told him that she still loved him very much. She asked if they could meet and talk.

"Eric," she said, "we have been separated for a long time, but I still think of you every day and I pray for you daily. I embraced Catholicism last year, you know, and this has made such a big difference in my life. I have done many things for which I must take responsibility and I have asked God to forgive me for what has been my part in all of this. Can you find it within your heart to forgive me as well?"

At first, he hadn't known what to say to her. He was lost for words, as he thought of how bizarre life was. He had been thinking about her a lot lately and now she has called him wanting to meet.

"I mustn't feel triumphant," he decided, "because that would be all about thinking that he had been right." There was no right or wrong in this. If they were to have any chance of reconciliation at all, it would have to be based on both of them being in the present moment and letting go of their past.

"I would like that very much Michelle. I do think we have a lot to talk about and it is difficult, if not impossible, to go on with my life without getting some sort of closure. How do you suggest we get together?"

"I am planning to drive to Toronto in a few weeks Eric, and I will phone you once I am settled."

He wanted to ask her where she planned to stay, but he caught himself just in time. *This was her decision. I must be careful not to fall into my old patterns of interfering,* he thought. *Don't take away her sense of accomplishment, this must belong to her.* His own sense of accomplishment had to come from his newly learned ability to become a more aware and understanding person.

He was eating his breakfast and simultaneously reading a book, as had become his habit, mostly because it took away the loneliness of eating by himself, when she phoned on a sunny Sunday morning several weeks later.

"Good morning Eric. How are you?"

"I am well, thank you. When did you arrive? I assume you are calling from somewhere in the Toronto area?"

"Yes Eric, I arrived several days ago. When can we meet?"

"My time is more or less my own Michelle, just tell me where and when."

"Actually, Eric, I am not too far away from your house. I came here for Sunday morning mass. I think you know where it is. You and I visited this small monastery once, when we where still together. It is a little past where your sister lives. Do you remember it? Why don't you come to the little chapel and meet me there in about an hour. Will that give you enough time to get ready?"

"Yes, it will only take me fifteen minutes to drive up there. So I will see you there at about eleven or so."

They hung up. He hurried to finish his breakfast and dress. He thought about all the previous unsuccessful times they had tried to meet in churches or chapels and he wondered out loud if God might be more kindly disposed now that she had converted to Roman-Catholicism.

He found her, kneeling and in deep prayers. He quietly slipped into the pew next to her and he gently put his hand over hers. She looked up and smiled her beautiful white smile, that smile which could disarm a roomful of contrary politicians. He looked into her eyes and knew that it was true what they said about eyes being the mirrors of souls. He recognized that they had their work cut out for them, and that they would have to work hard on their differences, but he also knew that he loved her very much and that she would undoubtedly teach him the things he still needed to learn, the things about patience and understanding and that with loving kindness his search would finally be over.

He decided that this really hadn't been a lifelong search for her, but instead a search for himself.